Look for More Titles by Cassandra Chandler

BRON
TARN
ROM

The Blades of Janus
PACK
PROGENITOR

The Forbidden Knights
FORBIDDEN INSTINCT

The Summer Park Psychics
WANDERING SOUL
WHISPERING HEARTS
LINGERING TOUCH
THE SUMMER PARK PSYCHICS OMNIBUS

Other Works
CRAFTING A WRITER'S LIFE: Building a Foundation

Coming Soon

The Blades of Janus
PERIHELION

Cygnian 7
ZAKARRI

Rom: A Scifi Alien Warriors Romance

Cygnian 7
Book Seven

Cassandra Chandler

Copyright Page

Rom: A Scifi Alien Warriors Romance
Cygnian 7, Book Seven
Copyright © 2024 by Cassandra Chandler
Print ISBN: 978-1-945702-99-0
Digital ISBN: 978-1-945702-98-3

First eBook edition: November 2024
First print edition: November 2024
10 9 8 7 6 5 4 3 2 1

cassandra-chandler.com
P.O. Box 91
Mission, Kansas 66201

Chapter One

Warm water dripped from Hayley's chin. Her head was pounding and the small shower cubicle seemed to spin. She leaned against the cold metal wall, letting the water rinse away the last vestiges of the soap she had used to get the disgusting tank fluid out of her hair and off her body.

"Hurry up in there."

She jumped at the brusque voice of the guard stationed outside. As quickly as she could, she finished rinsing, then turned off the water. Warm air blasted her from all sides, drying her quickly. Even her hair was left only a little damp. The artificial breeze ended and Hayley stepped outside, resting her hand on the wall to stay upright.

Why was everything spinning? Her joints ached as if she'd never used them before, her eyes were barely able to focus. She felt oddly disconnected from the pain. Nothing felt real.

She couldn't show weakness. Couldn't show anything at all. Nothing out of the ordinary, even though there was nothing ordinary about her life as it was now.

She had been abducted. Twice. Once by a shapeshifting

mercenary who had promised to protect her, but abandoned her with someone even worse than he was. Then by someone who had abducted her from her first kidnapper and taken her far from her homeworld. Someone who was using her for experiments that she didn't understand, but knew she had to do everything in her power to thwart.

Normal… Normal. Everything is normal.

Because when it wasn't normal, that caught his attention. Norem's.

She shuddered, forcing herself to walk the short distance between herself and the pile of clothes waiting for her. White panties, white sports bra, gray jumpsuit. The only clothing she'd seen in… How long had it been? She'd lost track. Her memory was foggy, even worse than usual.

Sophie. Amy. Becca. Buddy. David. Shannon.

She went through the names of her family of the heart back home. They had befriended her and her grandma when her own mother was dying of cancer, then they had taken her in when her grandma died a decade later. Hayley had only been seventeen. Now, she and the Myers sisters, Becca, Amy, and Hayley's best friend, Sophie, all lived in Hayley's family home.

Someday, she would see it again. Someday, she would see *them* again.

She had another family of the heart now. People she needed to help, that she *could* get back to, right now.

Others in a situation similar to hers.

As quickly as she could, she dressed, then stepped out into the corridor beyond the cleansing chamber. The Tau Ceti guard was waiting for her, wearing his form-fitting dark brown uniform. Three arcs of bronze metal curved over each shoulder and a matching bronze belt wrapped around his waist. A ray-gun was strapped to it. She knew better than to make a grab for it. These guys might look like something out of a cheesy, old-fashioned sci-fi movie, but they were fast, ruthless, and deadly.

He glared at her until she turned and started down the corridor. At least he didn't seem to find it odd that she was hunched over and walking slowly. Hayley's equilibrium still felt off. Norem would undoubtedly want to know that. It was probably a side-effect of whatever his most recent experiment on her had been. Mercifully, she couldn't remember what it was. She must have been unconscious for it.

A flash of memory assailed her. Bubbles bursting from her mouth as the breathing apparatus that sealed most of it and trailed down into her lungs was pulled out. Blue and green lights searing her eyes. Her skin burning and itching as if she was sunburned bad enough to peel.

"Keep moving."

The guard shoved her and she almost fell. She hadn't even realized that she had stopped to lean against the wall. What was wrong with her? This wasn't the same as the other treatments. Was it?

Her memory was so blurry, as if she were looking out through the liquid in her tank. Looking out at Norem, his long face distorted through the viscous fluid. His smile…

She shuddered again, but kept moving down the hall. Left foot, right foot. Left foot, right foot. Her joints felt odd and stretchy, as though the ligaments weren't used to holding everything together as she limped along down the corridor. The plain metal hall seemed to stretch on forever. Hayley wondered if she would ever see anything else. Finally, she arrived at the door to her cell. It slid open without a sound. She stumbled inside, barely making it to her cot before she collapsed.

There was no escape. Not even in sleep. Dreams assailed her. Swathes of blue were swirling in maddening circles. Cobalt and sapphire with streaks of silver that flew around her like ghosts.

"Hayley? Hayley?"

A soft voice edged around the corners of her mind. A voice of caring and love. The only comfort she would get in this hell.

"Where are you? I can't hear you anymore."

"Mindy?"

Even though Hayley couldn't see her friend, she could sense the huge dog wagging her tail happily.

"Hayley! Where did you go? You were so far away…"

"I'm sorry, Mindy. I… I don't know where I was."

Hayley did her best to shield Mindy from what had actually happened. She always did. The one blessing in this place was that Norem treated Mindy well. Hayley didn't want to risk that by letting him know that his MIN-D project was much more successful than he had imagined.

Norem wanted to connect Hayley and Mindy so that they could use each other as beacons in some kind of teleportation experiment. Hayley only knew that much because Norem spoke freely in front of Mindy, not realizing how much the dog understood—or that she could communicate everything he said to Hayley telepathically. Hayley was sure Mindy's intelligence was beyond anything Norem had expected and so was their bond.

Hayley had enough natural talent that she'd been able to hear Mindy when she arrived at his previous base on Ceres, back in her home solar system. Back near Earth. It was that innate ability that had first drawn his attention. A shudder passed through her.

"*You feel different,*" Mindy thought.

"*Different how?*"

"*I don't know. New.*"

New? Hayley didn't feel new. She felt ancient. Worn. Exhausted. She rolled over on the bed and stared at the plain bronze ceiling.

"*Rest now,*" Mindy thought.

"*Okay. You, too.*"

Hayley was only just starting to doze when a voice came through the speakers in her cell. This one was welcome, unlike when Norem checked in after a 'session.'

"Hey, stranger."

Hayley smiled despite everything. Tears flooded her eyes as relief coursed through her.

"Katie?"

"The one and only." After a pause, Katie said, "You were gone for a long while that time. You okay?"

"I'm great. Just like going to the spa."

Neither of them liked to talk about the tank. They had come up with their own little code words, trying to maintain their sanity through their absolutely insane circumstances.

"There was a hubbub while you were gone," Katie said. "Some sort of big transfer. I couldn't get details. Slime-o was absolutely paranoid about it and didn't put anything in the computers."

Hayley shuddered, even with Katie using their nickname for Norem. Another thing they had learned in their captivity was that the Tau Ceti had evolved from something akin to a frog. Cannibalistic frogs who ate the rest of their broodmates once they hatched, 'leaving only the strongest to survive.'

"You still with me, Hayley?" Katie asked.

"Yeah, sorry. This last round really wore me out."

"You know, it's funny," Katie said after a few moments

of silence. "You were gone so long, I thought maybe this time you weren't coming back."

"No way. You know our deal. We get out of here together."

"We get out of here together. Plus, the dog." Katie laughed.

"Plus, the dog." Hayley chuckled as well. "I just hope Slime-o hasn't brought in any new prisoners that we'll need to rescue when we make our great escape."

Katie was silent for a while again.

"Katie?"

"Yeah, about that... I was digging through the files again with these handy, freakish abilities that Slime-o managed to impart."

Whatever Norem had done to Katie had enabled her to project her mind into the station's computer systems. She was also a whiz with technology, though neither of them had access to anything remotely useful when they weren't under close scrutiny. Katie had been careful to conceal most of her abilities from Norem. In particular, the fact that she could secretly communicate with Hayley through the station's intercom system without anyone being aware. Katie had shared just enough of what she could do to keep her project 'active.' Neither of them knew what happened to the women who were part of projects that ended. All they knew was that they never saw them again.

"Please tell me he isn't bringing some other poor soul

to this hellscape," Hayley said.

"I'm not sure. There's mention of a new subject, but I'm not finding any recently created files. I don't understand it."

"I'd worry about you more if you did. Slime-o's mind remains a mystery."

"I guess that means the telepathy project he's working on with you is still a no-go?"

"Yeah. Yeah, that's a no-go." Hayley hated keeping secrets from Katie. Even with everything they'd been through, she wasn't sure who to trust—aside from Mindy.

Hayley closed her eyes and covered them with her arm, trying to block out the lights. She still saw sparks. Was she suddenly developing migraines? Great, that was just what she needed.

"I think I need to get some sleep," Hayley said. "Do you mind if we talk more later?"

"Not at all. I just… I missed you."

"I missed you, too." At least, Hayley was certain she would have, if she'd been conscious during the experiments. She wondered what Norem had done to her this time. A shiver went down her spine. Best not to think of it.

A short burst of static let Hayley know that Katie had disconnected their comms. Even though Katie's technokinetic abilities would probably be handier in an escape attempt, Hayley was grateful for her own telepathy that Norem had somehow activated—or rather, augmented. It wasn't just that she wasn't alone, but that she could be there for Mindy. She only wished she could see the dog in person and give her a big hug. Norem might be kind to the dog, but he wasn't the most affectionate guy. Mostly because Mindy kept biting him. She was a good judge of character, obviously.

Lights flashed against the backs of Hayley's eyelids again. She covered her eyes with both hands, but the light kept coming, each burst arriving more quickly than the last. She sat up and leaned her elbows on her knees, blinking quickly. The lights kept flashing.

Hayley stared around her small cell, unsure of what she was seeing. A line of white light appeared, hovering in the middle of the small room. She scrambled farther back on the cot, to where it was bracketed against the wall. There was nowhere for her to run to. Nowhere to hide.

The line of light expanded like a seam opening. Within, swirls of blue twisted around in mesmerizing patterns. Hayley leaned forward, almost willing to jump through and see if it led to freedom. Then she thought of Mindy and Katie, knowing she couldn't leave them behind.

A silhouette formed before her—a lighter blue that didn't swirl like the rest. Hayley couldn't tell if it grew larger or closer. All she could tell was that it was a man. He suddenly fell forward into the room. The light flashed once more, then vanished.

Hayley sat frozen on her cot, her chest heaving and her heart racing. The man was crouching in front of her, wearing eggshell-white pants and matching boots. Aside from a pair of chrome wristbands that covered a few inches of his forearms, that was it. A long row of serrated spines ran down the center of his back, resembling a stegosaurus, only dark blue. His skin was a lighter shade, as was the long hair that fell in front of his face, obscuring her view of his features. Beneath him, a pool of violet light illuminated the floor like the beam of a flashlight.

"H… hello?" Hayley said. "Are you okay?"

His dinosaur spine plates stiffened, becoming erect until they were standing straight up on his back. They began to flutter, then vibrate, blurring as would the wings of a hummingbird. They even created a low humming noise. It filled the room, washing over her skin and seeping through her tired muscles and aching joints. The vibration relaxed her, eased her pain, made her feel… real somehow.

Tingles spread up and down her spine, spreading out along her arms and legs. She felt her cheeks flush as other areas also heated, molten desire pooling deep in her belly. That vibration was… really something. The man slowly straightened, the muscles of his back rippling as he stood up and up and up. Her visitor's head nearly brushed the ceiling of her cell. He must be pushing seven feet tall. Hayley's jaw dropped when he shook his head, flipping his hair out of his face. He was unutterably gorgeous.

He had a square jaw, strong cheekbones, straight nose, and dark eyebrows over glowing violet eyes. His hair brushed his massive shoulders. Both arms were corded with bulging muscles, his chest and shoulders broad. Rows of abs were stacked on top of each other on his abdomen. He was absolutely ripped. His waist tapered, then flared out to narrow hips. She could clearly see the outline of his muscled legs through his pants.

Hayley thought she must have died. Men this perfect did not exist in reality. And even if they did, she certainly wouldn't react with so much lust and... longing for them.

"*Hayley?*" Mindy's voice suddenly appeared in Hayley's mind. "*Are you okay?*"

"*I am,*" she thought back, carefully walling off the feelings the man was generating within her from Mindy. "*I think I am.*"

"*You're more there.*"

"*What?*"

"*You're... more Hayley. More there. It's good.*"

"*I'm sorry, Mindy, I don't understand.*"

She heard a whining sound in her mind. Mindy didn't know how to explain better.

"*Don't worry,*" Hayley thought.

"*Someone is there.*"

Hayley didn't want to scare Mindy, but at the same time, if the dog could sense this guy, maybe she could help

Hayley figure out if he was friend or foe.

Who was Hayley kidding? He had appeared out of some kind of tear in the space-time continuum. He probably wanted to abduct Hayley again. Looking him up and down, she wasn't sure she'd object this time. Especially if there were no experiments involved. But he would have to take Mindy and Katie along, too.

"Can you read his mind?" Hayley thought.

"He's confused. It's all... blue. But, I like him."

That was enough for Hayley to get her racing heart under control. Her dizziness seemed to have disappeared and she realized she felt better than she had a moment before. Her spine was tingling weirdly, but compared to all the side-effects of Norem's previous experiments, that was nothing. Encouraged, she decided to be the one to make the first move. Again, really.

"Hi," she said.

He angled his head to the side as if he didn't understand her. Did he not have a version of whatever universal translator everyone seemed to use out here in space? He shook his head, weaving on his feet suddenly.

"Are you okay?" she asked.

He managed to steady himself. She noticed that he kept one fist closed. Not in a threatening way, rather as if he was holding something. He looked at it, then back to her.

"Who are you?" she asked.

He blinked a few times, the glow in his eyes fading a

bit till all she saw was their lovely violet hue. In a rich voice that sent tingles down her spine, he said, "Hayley?" Her stomach felt as if it had dropped through the floor. How did he know her name? He had to be working with Norem. What was his game, though? What did he want? She tried to keep herself frozen, not revealing any of her distress. He seemed to see it anyway.

"I won't hurt you," he said. "I would never hurt you."

"Who are you?" she repeated.

"I... I don't know."

"You know my name, but not your own?"

This had to be a trick. He was trying to get her to trust him. To reveal the secrets Norem undoubtedly suspected she was keeping. She wouldn't fall for it, even though the idea of having this guy for a huge, strong protector made her heart feel that it was breaking from the longing for it.

He looked at his hand and then held it out toward her. Slowly, he uncurled his fingers.

Light glinted off of a dozen charms. Charms she recognized.

Hayley gasped and slid forward, barely managing to get to her feet and stay there. Her knees were so wobbly, she would probably fall any moment. She cupped her hand beneath his, unable to look away from the bracelet. The man tilted his hand, letting the bracelet fall into her palms.

Hayley fell to her knees. She brought the charm bracelet to her face, tears flowing down her cheeks.

Blinking them away, she looked at each one, remembering the year that she and Sophie had exchanged them. The last one was the half-heart BFF charm. Its edge was bent where Hayley had used it attempting to pry open a panel back in the first cell she'd found herself in. The cell in the Sol system.

She looked back up at the blue man and shook her head. "How do you have this? Why are you here?"

"I don't know where it came from," he said. "I don't know who I am. All I know is that I'm here for you."

Chapter Two

The beautiful woman before him let out a harsh laugh. She clutched the bracelet to her chest just above her heart. The fear in her eyes made his breath hitch. The man wanted nothing more than to gather her into his arms and tell her that everything was going to be okay. From the wariness in her brilliantly blue eyes, he doubted she would accept his affection. He tried to satisfy himself by drinking in every detail he could about her

Vibrant copper hair framed her heart-shaped face. Her eyes were large, her nose delicate. Plump lips drew his attention and he had difficulty looking away. Her skin was porcelain-white. It had the bloodless appearance of spacefarers who didn't have a chance to bask in any sort of solar energy. He wondered if she had ever seen a sun from planetside and vowed to himself that he would take her to the most verdant paradise he could find.

He would do anything to ease the look of fear in her eyes. Anything to win her trust. He felt the twin beats of his heart grow closer to a synchronized beat, the rhythm somehow calling him to her with a force stronger than gravity. He didn't know who he was, where he was from, nor how he had arrived here. All he was certain of was that he belonged at her side. Protecting her. Caring for her.

Loving her.

"Your eyes are glowing," she said.

He lifted his hand to his face. A violet glow tinged the blue of his skin. Before he could say anything more, the single door to the cramped room slid open. Hayley quickly leapt to her feet, keeping him directly between the door and herself, while blocking whoever was behind him from seeing her. She slipped the bracelet into her pocket, then cast a pleading look at him and shook her head.

Who had caused such fear to haunt her eyes? His spine plates vibrated strongly. He would find the person responsible and tear them into pieces.

A startled gasp sounded behind him. He struck the metal wristbands on his forearms together, but couldn't remember what he was supposed to do next. There was something else. Something that would make them more useful. Dammit, why couldn't he remember? He turned, keeping Hayley behind him and shifting his feet to a fighting stance. He curled his hands into fists, ready to fight to defend her.

The man standing outside of the door could hardly be seen as a threat. A gaunt, hollow-cheeked man who was staring at them with wide eyes and a slack jaw.

"Rom?" the man said.

Rom.

Something in his mind clicked. That was his name. He was sure of it. How had this man known? Rom didn't like the idea of someone else knowing more about himself than he did.

"That sounds right," Rom returned. "But who the hell are you?"

"You don't know?" the man questioned. He seemed familiar, but not in a friendly way. That just made his next statement raise Rom's suspicions even more. "I'm your friend, Norem."

"Norem." Rom shook his head. "Doesn't ring a bell."

Norem's lips pulled into a wide smile. "Don't worry. It's just a side-effect of your brave journey."

"What journey?" Rom demanded.

"Why, you volunteered for a very dangerous scientific test." Norem shook his head gravely. "Not many would have had the courage to be the first to test our transit portal, but you knew you had a better chance of surviving."

As much as Rom didn't trust this guy, parts of what Norem was saying felt right. Rom *had* done something unknown and dangerous. And, he had believed he was protecting others from risk when doing so. The idea that he worked with this guy, though... Rom wasn't buying it. Still, until he knew more about what was going on, he would play along.

"We weren't sure you'd make your way back to us." Norem's eyes narrowed, as if he was staring through Rom's chest. At Hayley. His smile dimmed. "Interesting that you should end up here."

Rom straightened, sucking in a huge breath to expand his chest. He braced his arms at his sides as well, doing his best to block Hayley completely from Norem's view. Norem smirked, his gaze snapping to Rom's for a moment. Then his smile deepened.

"I'm so glad that you made it," Norem said. "And I can't wait to hear all about your experiences."

Even if Rom had information to share, he wouldn't do so with this man. He didn't want to admit the depths of his ignorance, either. He had a feeling things would go better with Norem if the man thought Rom was useful.

"I'm still a bit blurry on the details," Rom said. "I need some time to get my thoughts in order."

"Of course." Norem nodded thoughtfully. "In the meantime, I can still examine you. Make sure you really are okay."

"I'm fine," Rom said.

"It's always best to be sure," Norem said.

"I don't need an exam." Rom didn't like how much Norem was pressuring him about it.

"Well, then…" Norem shrugged. "I suppose that's alright. But I definitely need to examine the subject behind you."

Rom's spine plates increased their rate of vibration. He took in another deep breath, his hands clenching back into fists. Throughout this all, Hayley hadn't said a word. She had scarcely moved. It was as though she was hoping they would forget she existed.

Rom could never forget she existed. Even with his mind scrambled and his memories blank, he knew her. He remembered her.

"Hayley," Norem said. "If you would be so kind as to accompany me to—"

"She's not going anywhere," Rom broke in.

"Now, that could be a problem." Norem made a clicking sound and shook his head. "Hayley has very specific medical needs. If I can't examine her, I can't help her."

Rom was skeptical about this guy's idea of 'help.' At the same time, he didn't have enough information about Hayley's situation to know how to keep her safe. He turned to her, staring down into her wide blue eyes. The anguish and despair he saw there made his hearts stutter. Something else glimmered in their depths. Anger. Betrayal. Rom's chest ached as he could almost feel her emotions seeping into him. He wasn't sure how she thought he had wronged her, but he longed to understand and to make it right.

"Do you want to go with him?" Rom kept his voice as gentle as he could.

She didn't speak, but shook her head in a small, jerky movement. Her eyes widened and she looked past Rom to Norem, her lips tightening until they were bloodless. She was absolutely terrified of that man.

Heat built in Rom's chest. His spine plates seemed to be trying to fly off his back, they were vibrating so hard. Claws extended from the ends of his fingertips, but he ground them against his palms rather than let them be seen. Hayley's eyes snapped back to him and she gasped, her lips parting slightly as she stepped back. Her knees hit the edge of her bunk and she started to fall.

Rom instinctively sprang forward. It didn't matter that she was falling onto a bed—albeit, a very uncomfortable-looking one. There was a hard wall right behind it. And she was *falling*. He couldn't not try to help her. The room was so small, he barely had to take a step closer to be right in her space. He wrapped his arms around her, easily catching her slight weight before she could land on the bed and pulling her against his chest.

The heat in his chest bloomed to an inferno. It spread through his limbs, along his back, radiating through his spine plates. He could barely breathe. At the same time, he felt more alive than he thought possible. Every cell in his body responded to her touch, lighting up as if they were being charged with electricity that somehow didn't hurt. Her eyes widened further as she looked up at him, her cheeks turning pink. The flush spread down her neck as her arms wrapped around his waist.

Was she feeling the same thing? If so, it was a good thing they weren't alone, or things would be getting really friendly really fast. She licked her lips, and it was all he could do to suppress a groan. He wanted to kiss her, to pull her closer, to worship her body with his.

He needed to get himself under control. She needed his help, and for that to happen, Rom needed more information.

Drawing on every ounce of his self-control, he straightened, setting her on her feet. He couldn't bring himself to pull away from her completely and left one arm around her shoulder. She kept clinging to him as if her life depended on it.

Rom could feel a tremor passing through her. Was it just fear, or was there really something wrong with her?

"Listen, sweetheart," he murmured in a low tone. "It sounds like we both need to be checked out."

She stiffened, trying to pull away. Rom gently hugged her tighter for a moment, but then loosened his grip so she knew he wouldn't stop her if she truly wanted space.

"We go together," he said. "I'll be by your side the entire time. If the good old doc here does anything you don't like, I'll snap his neck for you."

She snickered, then sucked in her breath as if she was trying to pull back the sound. Rom let out a low chuckle. Even without his memory, he felt confident that he could do as he said. He had felt absolutely no fear since he'd arrived, only concern for Hayley. He might not remember particulars, but he knew deep within himself that he could throw down with anyone around and come out on top. He just had to be sure he could keep Hayley safe while he did so.

"How about it?" Rom said. "Let's stretch our legs and get out of this shoebox."

She nodded slightly, tucking herself closer into his side. They turned back toward the door, except before they could take a step, Norem shook his head and laughed.

"I see your reputation is well-earned," Norem said. "You do have a way with the ladies."

Rom's hearts beat more quickly, their out of sync pace making him dizzy for a moment. Hayley stiffened beside him. She didn't move away, but she dropped her arm from around his waist. That wasn't the worst of it, though. The worst was that yet again what Norem said sounded familiar. Rom somehow knew that it was true.

"I'm only interested in one," he said firmly. He looked down at Hayley and softened his tone. "I hadn't met you yet or I swear, I never would have—"

"Let's just..." Finally, she spoke, her tone as cold as the vacuum of space. "Let's just get this over with." She straightened, squaring her shoulders before walking toward Norem and leaving Rom behind.

He had hurt her. Maker, how could he have hurt her so

deeply that she would rather walk up to a man who absolutely terrified her than stand at Rom's side? She belonged there. He knew it with more certainty than anything. Rom rushed forward to walk near her. She had already turned down the corridor and was confidently striding ahead of them.

As Rom passed Norem, he heard the other man murmur, "Redheads are always trouble."

There was venom in the man's tone, evident even in the whispered comment. Rom hurried to catch up to Hayley. He didn't know what to say, but at least he could keep his promise to stay with her. It was a good thing, too, because she suddenly tilted to the side, her legs collapsing beneath her. Rom was right there, sweeping her up in his arms and nestling her against his chest.

"Hayley?" he said. "Hayley, are you alright?"

She shook her head, blinking her eyes blearily. "I'm just dizzy all of a sudden."

Rom looked to Norem. The other man shook his head and made a tutting sound.

"As I told you, she is unwell," Norem said. "Let's get her to the infirmary." He smiled broadly as he strode in front of Rom, leading the way down the hallway.

"Don't leave me alone with him," Hayley whispered so low Rom could barely hear. She clutched at Rom's chest. "Please, don't let him hurt me anymore."

Rage flooded him. He didn't think his spine plates

would ever lower again. What had Norem done to Hayley to make her so afraid? How had he hurt her in the past? Norem pretended to have her best interests in mind, but Rom could tell it was a sinister facade. Every instinct in his body told him not to trust the other man. At the same time, Rom didn't even know where he was, who he was, or what he might face if he confessed to knowing that Norem was his enemy. Rom couldn't risk taking a stand until he knew he would be able to keep Hayley safe.

He lifted Hayley so that he could nuzzle her ear and whispered, "Best to play along for now."

He wasn't sure if her quick intake of breath was from his words or his breath playing across her skin. His pants were starting to get too tight as his dicks stirred, his skin tingling with the urge to press kisses along her neck, to swing her around in front of him and walk over to the nearest wall and claim her.

Claim?

He shook his head, pushing away the distracting thoughts. Hayley needed help. He wasn't sure what was wrong with her, and he definitely shouldn't be thinking anything along those lines. Still, she relaxed more into his arms, her head listing against him and her eyelids fluttering closed.

Rom turned his attention back to Norem. They took several turns through the facility, but it wasn't long before Norem stopped in front of a large door. He turned to Rom and smiled that creepy smile of his.

"If you'll give me one moment," Norem said, "I can tell my staff to prepare for two patients instead of one."

"You can tell them just as easy in front of me." Rom glared at the other man. It was one thing to pretend to play along with this guy. It was another to let him prepare an ambush.

Norem's smile grew brittle, but he nodded. "I suppose so."

He pressed his palm against a bioscanner next to the door. It slid open, revealing a large laboratory. Not an infirmary. A laboratory.

There were beds along one wall, with scanner readouts above them, but the majority of the space was taken up by tables and cabinets filled with containers of various colored liquids. Some of them could be medicines, but others were clearly components for creating chemicals. There was also a large glass box with gloves within that you could put your arms into from the outside and a whole row of magnification devices on a counter built into the far wall.

"Impressive, isn't it?" Norem said. "This is where we prepped you for your dangerous journey."

That was an outright lie. Rom had never been in this room in his life. He was sure of it. But Hayley... She peered up from Rom's arms, shuddering when she saw where they were and quickly tucking herself closer against him. Norem saw the movement and his lips quirked up into a brittle smirk. Rom wanted to punch it off his face.

Norem led the way into the lab. Several men dressed in long, light brown lab coats leapt off their stools when they saw Norem, standing at attention. Their eyes drifted to Rom and Hayley and their mouths dropped open, eyes wide in shock. Norem might act as if they had expected Rom to show up, but he was certain that was yet another lie.

"Settle down, settle down." Norem waved his hands in a gesture of calm. He turned back to Rom and smiled. "I know it's exciting, but Rom has returned to us. His brave journey was successful. However, we don't have time to celebrate."

The men backed toward their stations, their eyes locked on Rom. One backed into a stool, knocking it over. Every single lab tech jumped as it clattered on the floor.

"Back to work." Norem's smile vanished as he looked around the room. "And you." He pointed at the man who was righting the stool he'd knocked over. The guy froze, his fear obvious on his features. Norem continued as if oblivious to his effect on his subordinates. "Make sure to spread the word that Rom is back with us." Norem turned back to Rom and smiled. "We don't want any unfortunate surprises."

"I appreciate that," Rom said, forcing his own smile in return.

Norem's eyes narrowed slightly and he angled his head to the side. After a brief hesitation, he swung his arm in a welcoming gesture, pointing toward the beds.

"Hayley's condition is very rare," Norem said. "I've been working tirelessly to help her pull herself together." He let out a low chuff under his breath, as if he'd made some sort of joke.

Rom was not amused. He headed to the beds, keeping Hayley tight against his chest. When he reached them, he didn't set her down. Instead, he turned and sat down on one, letting her rest on his lap. Norem lifted an eyebrow, but didn't say anything. Neither did Hayley, but her nails scraped against Rom's chest as she pressed herself closer, as if trying to get as far away from Norem as possible.

"Now," Norem said, picking up a device from a table near the beds. "Let's begin."

Chapter Three

Tremors wracked Hayley's body. She doubted it was from whatever treatments Norem had subjected her to most recently. She couldn't even remember what he'd done. Except, she did remember everything else. The trips to the tank. The needles and injections. The surgeries doing who knew what to her body. She shuddered as Norem approached. Rom held her tighter.

Some of her tremors subsided. He was warm and strong and had shown her more kindness than she'd experienced from anyone in however long she'd been there. At least, in person. She didn't understand why Rom was being so nice to her—or worse, why she felt drawn to him. That was yet another mystery in her life. She had enough questions. What she needed were answers. She doubted this blue giant would have any for her, given that he had to learn his own name from her enemy. How could she trust Rom when he seemed to be working with Norem?

Her biggest questions pushed up in her thoughts again. *How do I get out of here? How do I rescue my friends?*

Norem glanced at the handheld scanner, a gleam in his eye that made her stomach churn. Whatever results he was seeing had him excited. That didn't usually end well for his test subjects. Was Rom really one of them? He didn't seem too bothered about it if he was. She doubted his nonchalance would last long, especially when Norem set down his scanner and started tapping on the bracer on his left forearm. He moved toward her, a small yellow beam of light extending from the end of it.

She flinched back. Not on purpose, but by reflex. She knew Norem hated it when she flinched. She knew it was useless to try to resist. The problem was she also knew what that little beam of light was. How much it hurt when he passed it over her skin, leaving small, cauterized spots of burned flesh in his wake.

Rom lashed out and grabbed Norem's wrist. Hayley wished she could say that she didn't smile internally at the pained look on Norem's face or take a ghoulish delight in the cracking sounds his wrist made. Then she realized that the laser had to be hitting Rom's hand. He had covered it with his palm, also blocking much of Norem's bracer in the process.

"Look out," she yelled, reaching for Rom's arm to pull him from the danger.

He didn't budge. It was like trying to move a stone statue. The blue man also didn't make any sound of pain. The laser should have burned a hole through his hand. She looked up to find him staring down at her with those beautiful violet eyes. They were glowing. His spine plates were vibrating again, their humming sound somehow soothing to her as well as… stimulating.

What kind of alien was he?

He slid Hayley from his lap so that she was sitting on the table, then stood, effortlessly taking Norem with him. The Tau Ceti's feet dangled above the floor, his lips were pulled away from his teeth as he gasped, sharp canines extending that made her shiver and recoil.

Was he a vampire? She didn't remember Norem being a vampire. At least he'd never bitten her. She'd never seen those fangs, either.

"I just need to take some samples," Norem said, his voice tight with pain.

Rom turned back to Norem and flexed his hand. Norem grunted, the sound joining with the crunch of metal being crushed. The Tau Ceti gasped, the color leeching from his face and leaving it a pale green.

Rom leaned in close and hissed, "Not that way."

He released Norem, who stumbled backward, barely keeping his balance. The moment he was free, Norem pried the misshapen bracer from his forearm, letting it clatter to the floor. He pushed on his hand, hard, wincing at another loud cracking sound. He gasped in a breath, the lines of pain around his eyes subsiding much too quickly for Hayley's taste. He wiggled the fingers of his right hand, cradling his arm against his chest. Gingerly, he let it drop back to his side.

"Very well." Norem lifted a shaky hand—his left hand —to smooth down his hair. He finished composing himself, but Hayley didn't miss the pointed look he cast at her. "We'll forgo tissue samples for the moment." He bit out the last three words, making sure she knew that he would make getting what he wanted from her as painful as possible after this.

Let him try. Rom hadn't just protected Hayley, he had given her a view of something she'd never thought could be done. He had shown that Norem, too, could feel pain. Hayley wanted a chance to inflict some of her own. She'd never been a bloodthirsty type, but after the torture she'd endured from Norem, she wanted payback.

"*Hayley?*" Mindy's voice was suddenly in her mind, nearly panicked. "*Hayley, are you okay?*"

"*I'm fine,*" Hayley thought back, trying to calm herself —and failing.

"*There are no stars where you are.*" A whine accompanied the thought. "*No light.*"

"*I'm sorry.*" Hayley closed her eyes and took a deep breath, then let it out slowly.

Normally, she had to project her thoughts for Mindy to pick up on them. Hayley had used that to protect the innocent dog from much of the suffering Hayley had endured. She was too upset, too angry to hold them back.

She was too tired of fighting to hold on.

"Please don't leave me again," Mindy thought, the whine increasing. *"Please, you were so far away for so long and you only just came back."*

I was far away?

Hayley managed to keep that thought to herself. She didn't remember going anywhere. Had Norem taken her off the station while she'd been unconscious recently? She suppressed a shudder, wondering what other things he'd done to her when she was unconscious. One of the few mercies in all of this was that he'd never expressed any interest in her other than as a science project. Still, sometimes she woke up feeling... different. This time was no exception. It might even be the worst.

Mindy had told Hayley that she would sometimes disappear from their link when Norem took her away. The times usually coincided with bigger experiments. Experiments that involved the tank.

The tank...

At times, Hayley almost regretted telling Norem that she could hear Mindy, that she was the 'natural telepathic talent' that he'd been searching for. But then, Hayley thought of all the people she loved that she had helped to keep safe by sacrificing herself. She thought of Mindy and how alone the poor pup had been before they'd found each other. It gave Hayley the strength she needed to endure.

"I'm okay," Hayley thought.

A long whine came back through their connection. One of the doors to a side laboratory opened and a man in a pale green lab coat emerged. He glanced around the room, letting out a sigh of relief when he saw Norem.

"Sir, there's a problem with M-37," the man said.

"I'll be with you in a moment." Norem was still rubbing his right wrist.

"But, sir—" Before the man could finish his sentence, there was a scream from the open doorway, followed by a loud bark.

Hayley's heart seemed to stop, then started pounding furiously. Her head felt as if it was splitting with every beat. More screams, barks, and growls joined in with the chorus of drums her circulation system was playing in her ears.

"*Mindy*," Hayley thought.

"*I'm coming!*" Mindy thought. "*I'm coming for you.*"

"*No, you can't.*"

Her warning was futile. A fluffy white Maremma sheepdog bounded through the open door. The man who had just entered reached for the large dog, but she ducked between his legs. The canine was so huge, she knocked the lab tech over. Her paws scrabbled on the floor as she skidded, trying to find traction. More of the scientists lunged for her. Her teeth clacked together loudly as she tried to bite them, scaring some of them off. One of them lifted a stool over his head, running toward Mindy.

Panic seared Hayley's chest. She slid to her feet, desperate to get to Mindy, to protect her, but Hayley knew she wouldn't be fast enough. Of all the people in the universe to step in, Norem grabbed a vial of something from one of the tables and hurled it at the man holding the stool. The vial exploded against his chest, its viscous contents eating through his clothes in seconds. Screaming, he dropped the stool and instead started stripping, dropping his sizzling shirt on the floor. He stared at Norem with wide, terror-filled eyes.

"Don't lay a finger on her," Norem yelled. "Her life is worth more than all of yours combined."

Finally, Hayley could breathe again. She knew that Norem had commanded that everyone treat Mindy well, but hadn't realized the extent of his concern for the dog. Hayley was sure he saw her as an experiment—his most successful one, the way he treated her. And Hayley was extremely grateful for that. How much of what Mindy could do had Norem figured out, though?

Still growling, Mindy glanced around at the men backing away from her. Hayley had never seen her before—only felt their connection. She knew that Mindy was a Maremma because of their telepathic conversations. Mindy had excitedly told Hayley that everyone always mistook her for a Great Pyrenees, although she was more lithe and a little bit less fluffy than that breed. Now, Hayley stared across the room, thinking that Mindy was the most beautiful dog she'd ever seen in her life.

She covered her mouth with her hands, trying not to cry. If Norem saw how affected Hayley was by seeing Mindy, he might grow suspicious about the pair. Who knew what that would mean for either of them, what sort of experiments he might dream up to learn more. Hayley would never forgive herself if Norem started to experiment on Mindy the way he'd experimented on herself and Katie.

Mindy's ears perked up when she saw Hayley. She started barking furiously, her mouth opening in a wide doggie smile while her tail was wagging like crazy. Then she did the worst possible thing she could do. She ran toward Hayley.

The panic Hayley had felt before was nothing compared to this. Her chest seized up, her vision growing dark around the edges. She couldn't breathe. This was her worst nightmare realized. How could she possibly keep Mindy safe?

Before Mindy reached her, Rom stepped between them. Hayley lurched forward, trying to stop whatever was about to happen. Her legs were slow to respond and she nearly tripped over her own feet. By the time she'd regained her balance, Rom had dropped to his knees, facing the dog. His arms were outstretched as if he sought an embrace.

Mindy's smile grew broader. She bounded into his chest hard enough to flatten most people. Rom barely leaned back. Hayley had the impression it was more to protect the dog than himself. She had felt his strength, seen it on display with the laser. The way he held Mindy so gently made Hayley's poor punished heart ache.

"Hello there, sweetheart," he said, laughing as the dog licked his face, hands, and shoulders. "I'm happy to meet you, too. What's your name?"

For a second, Hayley wondered if Rom could hear Mindy's thoughts as well. Then she realized he was just being friendly with her.

"Is it Nancy?" he asked. "You look like a Nancy to me."

She huffed and let out a playful growl.

"Not Nancy?" he teased. "What about Crystal?"

Mindy barked at him and shook her head.

"That is M-37," Norem said. "And she is a very valuable research animal."

Rom petted Mindy's head, then rubbed her ears like a pro. Whoever he was, he'd definitely been around dogs before. The thought was as reassuring as how loving he was being. Hayley's heart finally began to slow, her tunnel-vision expanding back to normal. Her head was still pounding, but at least she didn't feel like she was about to keel over anymore.

"M-37." Rom scoffed, still talking to Mindy instead of Norem. "That's a stupid thing to call a... whatever you are."

"She's a Maremma," Hayley said. When Rom glanced

up at her, she added, "It's a type of dog from Earth."

"Maremma dogs are an uncommon breed." Norem angled his head as he regarded Hayley. "I had no idea you knew so much about dogs."

"I grew up around them," Hayley quickly covered.

"Indeed." Norem narrowed his eyes, before he turned his attention back to Rom. "She seems quite taken with you, which is excellent. None of us can get near her without getting bitten. I've had to regenerate digits several times from our interactions."

Mindy let out a chuffing laugh. Norem frowned at her.

Regenerate... Generate...

The word kept repeating in Hayley's mind, her vision flashing between the room she was in and another. She was back in the tank, looking out through the yellow-tinged fluid surrounding her. Norem was there, staring at her with that creepy smile. He turned as a man walked up to him and handed him a large cylinder filled with the same yellow liquid. Something was floating in it. Something that made Hayley quickly look away, screaming around the tubes in her throat. Bubbles blurred her vision as she looked at the other man. The other... Norem.

Two of them?

Hayley pushed away from the... whatever it was. It couldn't be a memory. It had to be a nightmare. It was bad enough that one Norem existed. She didn't know if her sanity could take there being more of him.

"Are you okay?" Rom reached up to clasp her hand, his other still resting on Mindy's thick coat.

Mindy inched forward, whining and licking her lips as she stretched her neck in an effort to get closer to Hayley. Norem knew Hayley liked dogs now. He knew that Mindy liked Rom. She prayed that was enough to divert his suspicions, because she wasn't strong enough to resist Mindy right in front of her.

Hayley dropped down and did what she had longed to do ever since this nightmare began, when the first voice of kindness had reached out to her back in her cell on Norem's base on Ceres. She pulled her hand from Rom's grip, even though she wanted to hold on to him as well, and buried it in Mindy's fur.

Hayley tried not to show how much it meant to her to hold the dog as she wrapped her arms around Mindy. She held back her tears, her lungs burning with the suppressed urge to let out a sob as she nuzzled her face against Mindy's neck. Her heart soothed its aching beat, her muscles relaxed. Hayley had to admit that part of that was feeling the kind giant placing his hand on her back, staying close, just as he'd promised. She sensed that he would never let anything bad happen to her, even though she knew she didn't dare trust that fantasy. Instead, she focused on the warm feeling of her friend in her arms.

Mindy didn't move, didn't wiggle excitedly or jump up

and down. She didn't even try to lick Hayley. Maybe she was trying to hide her reaction as well, sensing the potential danger should Norem's suspicions be raised. The dog just rested her head against Hayley's and let out a sigh, as if she needed this moment of connection as much as Hayley did.

"*It's nice that you're not far away anymore,*" Mindy thought. "*You feel like you again. Like Hayley before, but new.*"

Hayley before? Before what? Maybe she meant before the experiments that Norem had been doing. Hayley certainly didn't feel like the same person who had been whisked away from Earth by a shapeshifting mercenary. Although, why did Mindy keep thinking Hayley was new? It must be a miscommunication. Mindy was incredibly intelligent, but she still perceived the universe through a dog's eyes. The way she processed her experiences was different. There were some experiences that they shared, though.

"What…" Hayley's voice tightened as she thought of what she wanted to ask, uncertain if she really wanted the answer. "What have you done to her?"

"Nothing," Norem said. "M-37 is treated like the prize she is."

"Prize?" Hayley asked.

"The pinnacle of one of my very first projects." Norem beamed, unable to keep from bragging. It was a trick

Hayley had used on him before to get him to give away information—not that it was really hard to do. He was so confident she would never escape that he would often explain things to her when she asked. It had especially been true early on in her captivity. Any gaps in the information she gleaned were usually provided by Katie's digging into the computer system or Mindy listening to nearby conversations. No one watched what they said in front of the dog.

"M-37 is a terrible name for a dog," Rom said. He looked up at the door Mindy had emerged from. MIN-D was stenciled above it. "Mindy."

Mindy's ears perked up. She turned to him and barked, wagging her tail.

"You like that name better, girl?" Rom asked, scratching behind her ear. Mindy barked again and he laughed. "Then that's what we'll call you." He turned his attention to the Tau Ceti scientists working—or lurking—in the room. "Got that?"

No one dared to speak, but several who were looking their way nodded. Those who did quickly glanced at Norem, eyes wide with fear, then turned back to their workstations. Norem stood above them, his thin lips pulled in a deep smirk as he stared at the trio as though assessing their very souls. Hayley's stomach felt as though it was filled with lead. She had seen that speculative focus too many times.

Pain always followed.

Chapter Four

"Mindy is an excellent name for her." The smirk Norem had been throwing their way turned to a smile. Rom wasn't buying it. Neither was Mindy.

The dog growled low in her throat, glaring at Norem as if she'd like nothing better than to tear his throat out. Rom was starting to share that opinion. He still needed more data before he could act. From what he had seen and heard so far, and what his hearts were telling him, this man and everyone in the room was an enemy. Everyone except Hayley and Mindy.

Mindy whined and shifted closer, pressing her head against Rom's chest and scooting her backside closer to Hayley. The dog was so big, she nearly knocked Hayley over. Rom slid his hand farther across Hayley's back, helping her keep her balance. She cast a grateful glance his way. His hearts started pounding even from that little glimpse of her glacier-blue eyes. She was so beautiful. And, though her body had been weakened by obvious ordeals, her spirit was still strong.

His spine plates stiffened as he imagined what she

might have been through. Norem was acting as though he was her doctor, but Rom highly doubted that was true. The guy could put on a fake smile and force his voice to drip with sincerity, but his eyes were as cold as a killer's. The way he had thrown that vial of caustic chemicals at one of his men without hesitating rankled Rom, even though he had done it to protect Mindy. Rom doubted it had been done out of the goodness of Norem's heart.

The shock on the underling's face had been telling. The looks on the other scientists' faces were even more informative. Sure, they were startled to see someone get splashed with something that ate through his clothes and looked just as likely to dissolve his flesh. However, once that initial shock fled, their expressions vacillated between fear and resignation. They hadn't been surprised, really. That kind of behavior was within their expectations for Norem.

Norem was obviously the leader of this place, yet he treated his underlings like dirt. He called Mindy a 'prize,' as if she was a mere thing and not a sentient life form. A very intelligent life form at that. She reminded Rom of someone. Several someones. Their faces and names flitted at the very edges of his mind, but when he tried to bring up the memories, they vanished. Dammit, he needed to remember. Who was he? What could he do? And most importantly, how could he help Hayley?

Her reaction to Norem was the most damning. She was

utterly terrified of him. Rom was certain that he had never seen anyone so afraid before. What had Norem done to make her feel that way? What was her place among his crew? Rom had a feeling he would not like the answer.

Rom himself seemed to have a position of prominence. He would use that to keep Hayley and Mindy safe until he figured things out. Starting a ruckus before he knew more about how many men Norem had at his disposal, what sort of weapons and training they had, and what sort of base they were on didn't seem wise. Were they on a planet with a breathable atmosphere and a climate that wouldn't kill them outright? Was it a dome world that would limit their ability to survive? Or, were they on a space station, floating in the void, trapping them with these unknown men?

He needed answers before he could take action. In order to get those answers, he had to play along.

Hayley leaned against him, her breathing shallow. Rom looked over to her and his hearts stuttered. Her lips had turned blue and her eyes were unfocused. Something was wrong with her. As much as Rom hated to admit it, he needed Norem's help figuring it out. Rom scooped Hayley up with him as he stood, then carried her back to one of the medical beds. Mindy followed at his heels.

"What are you doing?" Hayley asked, her voice a low rasp.

"Sweetheart, I know you don't want to hear this, but

something is going on with you that we need to sort out."

Rom shook his head. "Even without my memories, I know I'm not a doctor."

Rom started to set her down, but she grabbed his arms with surprising strength. Her eyes went wide as she turned toward Norem.

"No, I'm fine," she said. "I'm okay, really."

"Now, now, my dear." Norem approached slowly. "Where is this behavior coming from? Rom is going to think we aren't good hosts."

"Hayley, look at me," Rom said, ignoring Norem.

When her eyes met Rom's, they sparkled with unshed tears. The sight nearly broke him. He wanted nothing more than to turn around and rip Norem's head off. But he couldn't. Not yet, anyway.

"I will be right here," Rom said. "I will not leave your side. I think we need him to check you out. Maybe even to fix whatever's going on."

"Rom…" Her voice was more a groan. Rom hated hearing her say his name with such pain and fear behind it.

"I'm right here." Rom set her on the bed so that she was lying down, but kept his face inches from hers. A tear spilled out of the corner of her eye as she closed them, pinching her lips together tight. He kept her hand in his, encouraged at the strength with which she squeezed it.

"Well, that was unnecessarily dramatic," Norem said, stepping closer. "Now that we finally have her where we need her, I can begin."

Rom watched closely as the other man pulled a cart closer. Norem lifted the cloth that was covering the implements on it. Before Rom even registered what he was seeing, his spine plates began vibrating, his claws pushing against his fingertips. He kept them sheathed, not wanting to risk harm to Hayley.

The cart was covered in all sorts of old fashioned medical devices. Blades, clamps, and laser-cauterizers. There were even needles in little pouches and synthetic tubing. No sonic emitters. No high-frequency vibrational healing amplifiers. All of this would be considered barbaric among Rom's kind.

Wait… His kind? Was Norem not Rom's kind?

Rom glanced at Hayley's hand in his. Not only was hers tiny in comparison, his was very, very blue and hers was kinda pinkish. The connection he felt to her made it seem as though they were the same, despite their physical differences. It was a feeling he didn't share in regard to the other males in the room. He was also a foot and a half taller than all of them—closer to two feet for Hayley. The man who had torn his shirt off was standing with his back to them and there was no sign that he had the plates that Rom could feel jutting out of his own spine.

Rom was sure that many species had a great variety in their physiology. He was also certain that whatever these people were, he was not. Despite their connection, he didn't even think he was the same species as Hayley. Physically, anyway. Something deep within him recognized her as something even closer than the same species. She was part of him. He didn't understand it. The more time they spent together, the more certain of it he was. And he would do anything to protect her.

"Any pain she feels, I'll visit on you a thousandfold," Rom promised, glaring up at Norem.

Norem only chuckled. "Very dramatic."

He lifted a vial filled with green fluid and pressed it into a dermal transmitter. At least he wasn't using those needles to infuse it into her body. Hayley's eyes snapped open, widening as she saw it. She tried to pull her hand away from Rom's so she could crawl up the table and get away from Norem.

"I don't want to be knocked out," she said.

Rom gingerly pressed her shoulders down, trying to calm her. "It's okay, but you need to calm down."

Mindy jumped up so that her front paws were on the bed and started barking at Norem and even Rom.

Rom turned to the dog and said, "Hey, hey. Not helping. Quiet down."

Mindy whined and lowered her head, licking Hayley's cheek. Hayley curled her arm up so she could press her hand against the side of Mindy's neck.

"Please, I don't want to be knocked out," Hayley repeated.

"No one's going to knock you out. I just don't want you feeling any pain while Norem does what he needs to do to make sure you're okay."

She let out a grim laugh, lowering both arms to her sides. "I can handle pain."

Rom ground his teeth together as he wondered what exactly had brought her to this point. He was certain Norem had something to do with it. Rom was going to tear his head off. Eventually. Just as soon as he was no longer of any use.

"Just please don't let him knock me out," Hayley said. "I want to know what's happening. I have to see what's going on."

Rom stared up at Norem. The other man's smile deepened for a moment, then his brow creased with concern.

"Of course, Hayley," Norem said, in a voice that should have been soothing, but sent ripples of unease over Rom's skin. "I have to take some blood." He extracted a needle from one of the pouches that was connected to some sort of fastener, then hooked it to a small vial. "You're going to feel a little pinch."

Her lip curled up in a brief sneer, but then she quickly pressed them together tightly and nodded. She kept her eyes riveted on everything Norem was doing. Rom forced himself to watch as well, though he felt that he might be sick when the needle went in. Hayley didn't so much as flinch. His woman was strong.

My woman... She's mine and I'm hers.

Rom had to look away. There was something so unnatural about seeing her skin pierced like that. Rom focused on Norem's face and Rom's hearts stuttered again. Norem's lips were a thin line, a muscle working in his jaw. His nostrils flared and his eyes rolled shut briefly. He opened them, obviously straining to maintain his focus. His tongue darted out, licking his lips, and Rom caught a glimpse of those long canine fangs again.

Mindy was growling loudly. Rom was grateful. It covered the very similar response coming from his own chest.

"Now, now," Norem said, his voice taut and high. "You don't want to distract me, do you?" He smiled at Mindy, then detached the vial and replaced it with another.

"Don't take too much," Rom said. "She's weak enough as it is."

"I'm not weak," Hayley snapped.

Rom grinned at her. "My apologies. You're right. You're the strongest woman I've ever met."

"I thought you'd lost your memory," she countered.

Rom shook his head and laughed lightly. "There are some things I'm still sure of. That's one of them."

"You seem to have hit it off." Norem smiled at Rom briefly, then turned his attention to the scanner. His brow furrowed, but then he smirked—an expression Rom was somehow already coming to hate.

An odd feeling of dread welled up within him. He didn't respond. Neither did Hayley.

"I can forgo drawing any of the other fluids, depending on what the scans reveal." Norem turned that fake smile on Hayley. He finished filling a third vial, then detached it and dropped it down a small hole built in to the medical bed. As he removed the needle from her arm, he said, "The more you cooperate, the better it will be for everyone."

Her lips tightened, and she narrowed her eyes at him. Norem's smile broadened as if the exchange held some hidden meaning that Rom didn't understand. There was too much that he didn't understand—yet. He would get his answers, though, and soon.

"What does she need?" Rom asked. He hated that he needed to depend on Norem for anything, but something was obviously wrong with Hayley. Rom had no idea how to help her.

Norem was staring at the monitor above Hayley. Her three dimensional body was displayed with various parts highlighted and flashing in different colors. Her brain and nervous system blinked yellow, her circulatory system orange, and most of the rest of her flashed an angry shade of red. Rom shifted closer, lifting her hand and holding it against his chest. Was she okay? This did not look okay. He reached out with his other hand and placed it on her shoulder, wishing there was more that he could do. Mindy leaned forward and licked Hayley's cheek briefly.

"Well, isn't that interesting," Norem said.

Rom could hear the smirk in Norem's voice, but couldn't peel his eyes away from the scanner. The areas where Rom was touching Hayley briefly flickered, then turned green. The green highlight spread out from her shoulder and the left hand Rom held. Even her side closest to him gained a green tinge. The flashing of the yellow and orange slowed near those areas as well.

"What the hell does that mean?" Rom murmured, more to himself than anyone else.

"What?" Hayley craned her neck, trying to see the screen. Even Mindy's ears perked up as she stared at the monitor, letting out a low whine. "What do you see?"

Norem glanced down at Hayley and patted her right shoulder. For once, she didn't recoil. Rom felt the repulsion for her. He reached over to rest his hand on that shoulder, forcing Norem's hand away. They both looked up at the scanner to see that area of her body also turn from yellow and orange to a pale green. The shoulder Rom had touched before started to flicker again, but not as badly as it had been.

"Fascinating," Norem said. "It would seem your new friend has a stabilizing effect on you."

"That's good, right?" Hayley turned her attention back to Rom.

"I would think so," Rom said.

Warmth spread through him that she was looking to him to work through this, not Norem. It chilled him as Rom thought of how little he could actually do to help her. Then again, based on what the scanner was showing, maybe he *could* help. It would involve touching a whole lot more of her and he didn't know for how long. His spine plates had settled somewhat, but they started to vibrate again for an entirely different reason. The idea of touching her, of being close to her, made his skin prickle with awareness and blood start to pool in his belly.

Her cheeks turned pink, the flush spreading down her neck and her pupils dilating. She swallowed hard, the movement along her neck calling Rom's attention. Was she feeling the same attraction to Rom that he felt toward her? He pushed away the thought, forcing his body to calm. Hayley had just been through something. She was *still* going through something. Rom would do anything he could to be there for her. Now was not the time for anything more than focusing on getting her well.

"Well, isn't that interesting." Norem chuckled.

Rom followed Norem's line of sight to the monitor. More of the flickering lights were changing to that calm pale green. Lights around areas Rom was certain Hayley would rather keep private. Without thinking, he released her shoulder and slammed his fist into the screen. The material shattered as though it was made of nothing more than a thin, brittle layer of selenite. Sparks flew out of the display.

Rom quickly spread himself over Hayley, releasing her hand so he could pull Mindy under his chest as well and shield them both. He felt little motes of energy skitter over his back, but not anything that bothered him at all. Meanwhile, Norem leapt back, screaming as he furiously patted out an area on his sleeve that had caught fire.

Breathing heavily, Norem glared at Rom. "Well, things certainly have become eventful now that you've made your way back."

Chapter Five

The crackling sound of something electrical shorting out flooded Hayley's ears. It was accompanied by the caustic smell of burning wires. She heard several bursts of air above her and felt a wave of cold, the scent shifting to something more chemical. The crackling subsided.

Mindy was at her side. The dog was pressing her head against Hayley and whimpering, the front half of her furry body on the table with her friend and her back paws still on the floor. And above them both was Rom, shielding them with his glorious blue body. Hayley wanted to reach out and touch him. To explore the hard planes of his chest, the rows of his abs, those fascinating spine plates that always seemed to be protruding from his back.

What is wrong with me?

Hayley was in this mess in the first place because of a guy. She didn't know if she'd ever be able to trust her judgment in men again.

"Rom is different." Mindy must be picking up more of Hayley's thoughts than she realized. She did her best to put her shields back in place.

"*How is he different?*" Hayley very carefully broadcast the single thought.

"*He's the same,*" Mindy replied.

"*The same?*" Hayley tried to pick through what Mindy was communicating. It was sometimes hard to understand each other, with how differently they experienced the world. "*The same as what? As Dean?*"

Mindy let out a whine as Hayley's fear and despair at thinking about Dean leaked through their bond. She tried to block off that part of her, to protect Mindy, but it was hard. Dean was the cause of all this suffering. At least, Hayley's suffering. Mindy had already been with Norem when Hayley arrived, possibly for years. And Katie was on the station when they were both moved out of the Ceres base. If it weren't for Dean leaving Hayley with Norem, she would never have met the pair. They were the only bright spots in this horrible nightmare. Well, they had been. And now Rom.

"*I'm sorry,*" Hayley thought.

"*Rom doesn't hurt.*" Mindy broke into their dialogue more aggressively than usual. "*Rom helps. Rom heals. Rom is Hayley.*"

How could Rom be Hayley? That didn't make any sense. Aside from the fact that they were two different people, they weren't even the same species. He was a big blue giant from who knew where and she was an Earthling. Hayley didn't understand why Mindy thought they were the same.

Hayley looked up to see Rom staring at her with those beautiful violet eyes. They were glowing, concern etched on every inch of his face. Concern and something else. Something softer and more intense at the same time. Something that made butterflies flutter in her stomach and chased away the aches in her joints, warming her, making her feel… whole.

"*Rom is Hayley,*" Mindy repeated. "*Hayley is Rom. Different outsides, but the same inside.*"

Hayley still didn't understand what Mindy meant, but somehow, in that moment, it didn't matter. The three of them were together. Hayley didn't dare ever think that she was safe, but this was as close as they were probably going to get. As long as Rom was with them, he would protect them. She was sure of it.

I can use that…

She hated herself for thinking it. What other choice did she have, though? If it was only her own life on the line, she might resist. But she had to think of Mindy and Katie. Rom was their best hope of escaping this nightmare. Hayley couldn't pass up the chance to use it. To use *him*.

She reached up with a shaky hand and cupped his cheek. His eyes drifted shut and he lifted his hand to hers, pressing it more firmly against him. She wanted to rise to his lips. To kiss him. But she was too weak to even raise her head. He opened his eyes and smiled, so gently, it was as if he could read her thoughts as clearly as Mindy, and was telling her it was all going to be okay. Hayley's heart beat faster as part of her began to believe it.

"I need you to move her to another bed." Norem's harsh voice broke into their moment. A moment Hayley had intended to be a ruse, but ended up feeling so real.

Rom lifted his head to glare at Norem and growled. "And I need you to back the fuck off."

Hayley burst out laughing. She couldn't help it. The only person she'd heard swear in a long time was Katie, and that was one of her friend's favorite words. Somehow, hearing it from Rom made Hayley feel more at home. He almost sounded like Buddy, her chosen brother from back home. Everything about Rom felt like home.

He stood and scooped Hayley into his arms again, backing away from the table. Mindy somewhat clumsily managed to get all four paws on the floor again. She was glaring at Norem, growling. Rom let out a high whistle that had her ears perking in his direction.

"Come on, girl," Rom said.

Mindy's mouth dropped open into a doggie smile as she barked once, then trotted over to stand at his side.

"He feels like home," Hayley thought.

"He is your home," Mindy responded.

Rom turned and strode toward the exit.

"Where do you think you're going?" Norem demanded.

"To my quarters," Rom said. "I'm sure one of your

lackeys can show me the way."

"You can't just leave with my test subjects," Norem said.

Rom tensed beneath her, his muscles amazingly becoming even more firm. "'Test subjects.' *Subjects.*" He emphasized the plural at the end.

Norem didn't miss a beat. "If your brain hadn't been scrambled by blue space, you'd remember that this is a science station. We're conducting top secret research that will reshape the balance of power in the galaxy for millennia to come."

"In your favor," Rom said.

"In *our* favor." Norem corrected, shaking his head. "You volunteered to be a test subject yourself. Rom… You have to trust me. So many people's lives depend on it."

Hayley had to admit, Norem sounded convincing. Partly because he was speaking the truth—his words just held a different meaning beneath the surface. Lives depended on Rom trusting Norem. Katie's life. Mindy's life. Hayley's life. She held her breath, wondering whether Rom would see through Norem's act. What would happen if Rom did? They were outnumbered, isolated. There was no way he could keep both herself and Mindy safe, let alone help to rescue Katie.

Hayley looked up at Rom and said, "You have to trust him." She turned to Norem. "I understand how things are. We'll cooperate. Whatever you need. Just… let us stay together. Please."

Norem's scowl slowly pulled into a smile. "That's very wise of you, Hayley. I suppose it could be arranged."

"What's to arrange?" Rom asked, a challenging edge to his voice. "I'm taking her to my quarters."

"You don't normally have company." Norem's smile stiffened, but he didn't miss a beat. He turned to one of the scientists cringing nearby and said, "Take Rom to his quarters."

"Sir?" the man said in a shaky voice.

"Level 3, room 485." Norem glared at the man as if he could set fire to him with his eyes. "He'll need bowls for *'Mindy's'* food and water, as well as provisions for her. Make sure it's set up before you arrive."

"Yes, sir," the man said, hurriedly murmuring something into his bracer.

As the subordinate scurried toward the door, Norem called after him. "Be sure to send plenty of provisions for Hayley as well." The smile he cast at her turned into a leer. "She needs to keep her strength up."

Hayley felt her cheeks heat. Was that what Rom had in mind? In another world, she would be absolutely okay with that. She wasn't the type to throw herself at a guy— that was more her best friend, Sophie's, mode of operating. But Hayley had watched Sophie enough to know a few things about coming on to people. Hayley didn't have that much experience with guys, though. She wanted an emotional connection before anything physical happened, and it was hard to find partners who agreed with that.

Dean had seemed to be one of them, but then, look at where dating him had landed her. Her judgment was absolutely suspect. She'd had misgivings about Dean— misgivings that she had ignored at Sophie's urging—but if things hadn't gone off the rails as horribly as they had, she probably would have ended up in a serious relationship with him. How could she trust herself now?

Hayley shook herself internally, her thoughts spiraling. This was her situation now. For whatever reason, this blue giant seemed interested in protecting her—and Mindy. If Hayley could get him more attached, maybe she could convince him to protect Katie as well. Maybe she could get him to help them all escape.

She leaned closer into the wall of chest he provided. God, it felt good. Not just physically, but... She already felt as if they had a connection. How was that possible when they'd just met? It must be part of his alien-ness. Amy would say he was putting off some kind of pheromone that was affecting her. If so, Hayley was sure she was affecting him, too. Could she really use that to her advantage? Given how much was at stake, she didn't see any other options.

Rom curled his arms, shifting her closer against his chest. "You need anything else?"

Norem's eyes flicked to Rom's. "I thought you were

impatient to leave."

"I don't want us to be disturbed," Rom said.

Norem smirked. "I imagine not."

Hayley felt Rom's slight intake of breath. His arms stiffened around her. Though he might be feeling drawn to her as she was to him, it was very evident he did not like Norem's innuendos. The thought of it made her like Rom even more. An alien gentleman. Who would have thought?

"You took samples from her," Rom said. "I'm a 'test subject,' too."

Norem's eyes widened briefly and his lips parted. For a moment, he looked at Rom as if he was Christmas and his birthday and a trip to the amusement park all put together. He seemed to catch himself, a lot more obviously this time, and cleared his throat, looking away. He plastered a smile on his face once more when he returned his attention to them.

"I can see how eager you are to have a little time to yourselves," Norem said. "I can get what I need from you later."

"Sure." Rom's voice dripped with sarcasm.

Rom needed to work on his poker face. It was obvious that he hated Norem. Knowing all the tortuous things he had done to his own people, Hayley wondered how Rom could dare to be so openly antagonistic. Were they working together or not? Hayley almost started to think that Rom might be under some form of duress to participate in Norem's experiments. She would have to ask Rom the first chance she had. Which, apparently, wouldn't be long.

He turned and headed toward the door, with Mindy following along behind them. It slid open at his approach. The man who Norem had instructed to take them to Rom's quarters was waiting just outside. He jumped when he saw them, but then sort of half-bowed. Mindy let out a low growl, staring at him.

"This… way…" he said, his eyes riveted on Mindy.

He led them through a maze of bleak corridors to an elevator. Hayley snorted as she felt the inertia of the room starting to move.

"Something funny?" Rom asked gently.

"No elevator music," she said. When he stared at her quizzically, she added, "On Earth, we often play music in our elevators."

"Hmm." Rom nodded, his lips pulling up in a lop-sided smile. "Sounds nice."

"It would be, except the music has been reworked so that it's as unobjectionable as possible," she said. "It's just kind of tepid."

Rom chuckled. "I like the vocabulary."

"I'm a writer," she said brightly. Her heart seemed to stutter and a chill swept over her. Her voice lowered, all the animation gone. "I was a writer."

Rom hugged her closer. She felt something brush the

top of her head. A kiss? If so, it had been nothing more than a comfort. Some of the warmth returned to her.

"That kind of thing doesn't go away just because you're not doing it," he said. "What did you write about? Spicy Romances with happy endings? Those are my favorite."

She smiled at the thought of this goliath reading Romances. When she looked up at him, his expression was open and earnest. He hadn't even been joking.

"When have you had a chance to read Romances?" She laughed.

"I have a friend who runs a library," he said. "She's always recommending—"

He cut himself off quickly, shaking his head. She felt him sort of list to the side, but he caught himself before falling.

"Sorry," he said. "I think I was confused there for a minute. What were we talking about?"

This guy really needed to work on his poker face. It was painfully obvious that he was trying to cover for what he'd been saying a moment before. If that was a memory resurfacing—hanging out with a librarian—she liked this guy even more. Hayley did her best to help him out.

"You asked what I wrote," she said. "And the answer is that I was—I am—a travel writer. I visit places and then write about them for people who either want to go there or who enjoy exploring places in their minds."

"That sounds nice," he said.

The elevator doors opened and the man practically leapt out. Rom probably needn't have worried about the Tau Ceti deducing anything about his slip-up. All the guy seemed to want to do was get them to their destination and then run like heck the other way. The idea amused Hayley more than it should. This guy had been part of her suffering. Part of so many others' as well. But that didn't mean she should take delight in his emotional trauma. She was just… enjoying the sense of justice being served.

Sure, that's it.

They navigated a few short halls with doors on either side. The lab tech suddenly veered to the side just as a door opened. Another lab tech ran out and the men slammed into each other with a loud, "Oof!" Hayley tried not to snicker. Mindy let out a loud bark, her tail wagging. Both men shrieked, holding onto each other as if for dear life.

That was too much. Hayley busted out laughing. She kept laughing as Rom carried her into the room, crowding past the two men who were still clinging to each other and walking sideways, trying to get out of the way and not trip. Mindy darted inside and immediately leapt onto a huge bed across the room.

Hayley stared at the opulent room surrounding them. There were no windows, but another door stood open on the left wall that led to a bathroom. She thought she caught a glimpse of an actual tub inside. The idea of sliding into hot water and letting all her aches and pains fade away enticed her. When Rom joined her, the water level would rise so much, it would slosh over onto the floor.

She blushed yet again at the thought, quickly looking away from the room. Her eyes landed on the bed, of course. Wow, that was a big bed. It could easily fit all three of them. Or maybe Mindy could check out the bathroom for a little bit while Hayley and Rom...

"*I can go...*" Mindy's thoughts were tentative in Hayley's mind.

"*No, please stay.*" Embarrassment washed through her. "*You didn't hear what I was thinking just now, did you?*"

"*No, but I can smell things.*" Mindy pushed her nose into the bed's comforter for a moment, then lifted her head and opened her mouth, her tongue lolling to the side as if she was laughing. "*You like him.*"

"*I do, but that doesn't mean I want you to leave,*" Hayley said. "*Especially not because of... that.*"

Mindy let out a chuffing sound. Hayley couldn't blame her. She barely believed herself.

Her misgivings only grew worse as Rom leaned toward the men outside menacingly and said, "We are not to be disturbed."

The door to the chamber slid shut.

Chapter Six

Rom was surrounded by enemies. The more he and Norem spoke, the more certain Rom became that the people working on this space station posed a grievous threat. He just couldn't remember what was in danger. The only thing he knew for certain was that Hayley and Mindy were in immediate jeopardy and that he would do everything in his power to keep them safe.

He didn't feel as though he was in danger himself. That was odd. Sure, Norem was trying to pretend they were friends, but Rom wasn't buying that 'Old Buddy' act for a moment.

Buddy…

Wait… Rom knew someone. A real friend. A buddy. Someone named Buddy?

Rom shook his head as another wave of dizziness assailed him. He hated to be even a few feet from Hayley, but he needed for her to be safe from himself as well. If he fell and landed on her, she'd be crushed beneath his weight. He strode over to the bed and set her down. Her arms quickly rose to his neck, keeping him close.

"Where are you going?" The panic in her eyes tore at his hearts.

"Nowhere." He gingerly unclasped her arms and pulled them away. "As much as I want to stay at your side, I need to check out the room. But, I'll be right here. Okay?"

She nodded, her lips pulled in a tight line. Mindy crawled up the bed making odd, silly grunting noises. Hayley finally burst into a smile. The dog managed to get as close to Hayley as she could, then flopped on her side. Hayley buried her fingers in Mindy's coat, hugging her close.

"See, Mindy here will keep you company," Rom said. Hayley looked up, fear suffusing her expression once more. Rom whispered, "I'm not going anywhere," and squeezed her hand.

She nodded, her eyes glittering with unshed tears, then turned her attention back to Mindy. Rom stepped away quickly. The speed made it slightly easier to move away from her, as well as shielding her from his building rage at Norem.

What the hell had Norem done to her? She was weak as a kitten, her skin looked bloodless, even though the 'scientist' hadn't taken all that much. The worst part was that she was terrified of just about everything.

Despite that, Rom could sense an inner strength within her. She would do anything to protect Mindy, for one thing. She had played it cool with Norem, but Rom had detected it, like a faint echo. It was up to Rom to keep them all safe and get them out of here. He just had to figure out where they were, where they should go, and how they could manage it all.

Yeah, just that.

He needed to remember who he was. At the same time, he doubted that Norem would be so accommodating once Rom came right out and let him know they were enemies. No, Rom needed to keep up the act for as long as possible. He needed to talk to Hayley, to get more information. Except, before he did that, he had to know if Norem was listening in.

On the surface, the room looked like standard quarters for an officer. It was a bit small for Rom's tastes, and the color scheme was downright dreary. He was accustomed to more light. Light and rainbows. A memory teased the surface of his mind. Milky white crystal with waves of iridescence flowing through it. The image brought a sense of home and belonging that made his hearts ache.

"Are you okay?" Hayley asked.

"Yeah. Yeah, I'm fine."

How did she know something had been off with him, even for a moment? His expression hadn't changed, he was certain. Was it possible that she was feeling the same echoes of his emotions as he was feeling for hers? He filed that information away, bringing his focus back to the task at hand.

All the furniture was bolted down. That was a bad sign, pointing to them being in space rather than planetside. Rom would like their odds a lot more if he knew he could smash through a wall, throw Hayley over one shoulder, Mindy over the other, and tear off into the wilderness. Instead, punching a hole in the wrong wall could decompress the room they were in. He had a strange feeling that he would be fine, but Hayley and Mindy wouldn't. He couldn't jeopardize their safety.

Rom found a closet and started rifling through the uniforms within. They were all identical to the brown with bronze accents uniforms that the rest of the soldiers wore. Soldiers. Not scientists. Interesting that his brain should pop that word into his awareness. It seemed to fit, though.

They hadn't passed anyone on their way to these quarters. Rom was certain that it had been intentional. Whether it was a station or a ship, being in space meant compact living to conserve resources, especially for sentients who had to construct their ships out of manufactured materials like this rather than growing them from crystal.

Wait, was that what he'd seen before? The vision of the milky white crystal came back to him. Was that his real home? His ship?

"You won't find it," Hayley said.

"Find what?"

"Evidence that these are your quarters. I doubt you've

ever been here before."

"Now, what would make you say that?" Rom pulled out a uniform and held it up in front of himself. The pants and sleeves were several inches too short. Hayley laughed, as he'd hoped she would. "Maybe I grew a little on my travels. I could still squeeze into this."

"Turn it around," Hayley said. Rom flipped the garment so she could see its other side. She shook her head. "There's no accommodation for your... spine... thingies."

"My 'spine-thingies?'" He chuckled. "Spine plates. And they don't always have to be up."

He turned around and willed his spine plates to rest against his back. It took some doing, considering how worked up he still was, but he managed.

"See?" he said.

"Wow, that is cool."

He turned back to her, smirking as he took in the way she was ogling him. Then he noticed that her skin had that sickly bloodless look again and had taken on a waxy cast. He threw the uniform back in the closet and hurried over to her.

"You need to rest." He helped her lay back against the pillows, fluffing them up beneath her.

"It's okay. I'm okay."

She absolutely was not okay. Rom lifted her hand in his. Her skin was ice cold and clammy, with a bizarrely smooth texture that made his spine plates rise again.

"I'll get Norem." He started to rise but her grip tightened.

"No! Please, don't. I'll be fine. I just need a minute."

Rom leaned forward and swiped some hair away from her forehead. Beads of sweat had appeared, then even as he watched, they faded back into her skin. That didn't seem right. Something was seriously wrong with her. Lights glinted on the shiny wristbands he wore, only inches away from Hayley. He was certain that they possessed technology that could help her, if only he could remember how to use them.

"I feel so useless," he said. "I know if my memories returned that I could help you."

"You are helping me." She smiled softly, her eyes closed. "Whenever you're close, wherever you touch me, I feel better."

Something stirred within him. He could feel his heartbeats changing, their alternating cadence coming closer together. Closer to... one-ness? Joining? Why couldn't he remember? He knew it was important. She was important. She was his world.

"Why is it that I can't remember anything about myself, and yet I feel as if I know you?" Rom said. "As if I've known you my entire life."

She chuckled. "I think I would remember meeting a giant blue warrior from outer space."

"I guess so," he said.

Closeness helps her. We need to be closer.

For some reason, the image of two swirling, chaotic balls of light popped into his mind. They drew closer, merging into one beautiful orb of energy. His eyes burned and his chest felt overfull. Why wouldn't his brain just let him remember who he was and how he could be useful?

"Hayley, look at me," he said. When she opened her eyes, he leaned closer. She let out a breath as if even that eased whatever was happening to her. "I will never hurt you. I will protect you. Can you trust me? At least a little?"

After a moment, she nodded.

"Alright." He nodded back. "If me being close helps you out, then I'm going to get closer. I swear to be a gentleman."

Her eyes widened and she sucked in a breath. Pink flooded her cheeks. She was so pallid, the contrast was glaringly obvious whenever she blushed. Was that disappointment he saw at the corners of her mouth? He was probably projecting. In any case, he had to focus on getting her better before he thought of anything else.

"I'm going to lie next to you," he said. "Is that okay?"

This time, she nodded without a moment's hesitation. He tried to hide his smile but failed.

"Well, alright then," he said. "Mindy's right there to act as a chaperone."

Hayley laughed. "I feel like we're going to a high

school dance."

"I have no idea what that means, but if it makes you laugh, I'm good with it."

As gingerly as he could, he slid his body next to her, wrapping his arms around her and holding her close. He pressed his bare chest and stomach to her side, his legs to hers. His skin prickled with awareness, heat flooding him wherever they touched skin-to-skin. It was both ecstasy and torture—he never wanted to let go.

Hayley let out a deep sigh, relaxing against him. More color seemed to be seeping back into her skin. The weird waxy texture also vanished after a few moments. What the hell was wrong with her and why did his proximity help? Maybe it wasn't him. Mindy was plastered to Hayley's other side.

"Better?" Rom asked gently.

"Mmm." Hayley smiled, her eyes drifting shut once more.

"Then you just rest. I'll be right here when you wake up."

She shook her head and forced her eyes open, starting to rise. "No, I can't sleep."

Rom urged her to stay lying down. "It's okay. I'll protect you."

She let out a snort that was somehow full of despair. "You can't protect me. No one can. Not even Dean."

Rom's spine plates rose, vibrating against the mattress.

He lifted himself on his elbow to give them room while staying as close to Hayley as he could.

"Why does that name make me want to start tearing the room apart?" Rom asked.

"Because he's the guy who left me with Norem." Hayley shook her head.

"I already hate him," Rom said.

She let out that deadened half-laugh again. "You're not the only one. I can't believe how foolish I was. I thought he cared about me."

Rom's hearts stuttered. "Did you care for him?"

"We dated for a couple of weeks," she said. "We hadn't gotten serious or anything yet. Then, when we wanted to, he told me the truth about himself. That he was an alien. I should never have agreed to get on his ship, but you know —travel writer." She shook her head. "He told me it was going to be the greatest adventure of my life. Then he left me with Norem and vanished."

Rage tore through Rom. He wanted to find Dean and tear him to pieces. But it didn't seem right to expose Hayley to that kind of violence and rage. She had been through enough already.

"I'm so sorry that happened to you," Rom said.

"I want to believe that things happen for a reason." She buried her fingers in Mindy's fur and the dog's tail thumped the bed. "I wouldn't have found Mindy. She wouldn't have someone to look out for her and keep her company."

Mindy looked up and opened her mouth. Rom thought she was about to say something, but all that came out was a little bark. Couldn't animals talk? He would have sworn they could. Mindy crawled closer to Hayley's face and started licking her cheek. Hayley's eyes brightened for a moment, then she smiled and shook her head. It was almost as if the pair were having a conversation that Rom couldn't hear.

Wait, hadn't they just met? Rom tried to think over what Hayley had said back in the lab. It had sure seemed to Rom as if they hadn't known each other before. Now Hayley was talking as if they were old friends. It was yet another puzzle for him to sort out. For the moment, he was just glad that Hayley looked as though she was feeling better. Her cheeks had more color and her breathing was more regular. Rom didn't know if whatever she'd been dealing with was passing or whether it really was his proximity making her feel better. Either way, he wasn't going anywhere.

"How did Norem know your name?" Hayley kept staring at Mindy as she spoke.

"I don't have a good answer for that," Rom said.

"How about the truth?" She turned to him, her eyes filled with bitter defiance. No matter what she felt because of his nearness, she didn't trust him. Rom couldn't blame her.

"We know each other," Rom said. "Actually, know of each other. And that's why I know that this room has to be rigged with all kinds of surveillance. Hell, he's probably watching us and listening to us right now."

"I just need to know if we're friends or enemies." Her voice was stronger than before, filled with a challenge that sent a pleasant shiver over his skin. Rom reached up and cupped her face with one hand.

"You are my everything. I will do anything you need. Be anything you want. All you have to do is say the word."

"I want you to kill every Tau Ceti on this station."

His hearts seemed to freeze in his chest, the coldness of her tone, of her request, chilling him to his soul. He lowered his head and closed his eyes as a wave of utter emptiness flooded him.

"I guess I have my answer," Hayley said. "You don't want to do it."

"I don't want to think about what must have happened to you that would make someone with such a good heart want me to do such a terrible act." Rom shook his head. He looked back to her and swept his thumb across her cheek. "It's as good as done. They're all walking ghosts. I just need to figure out how to keep you and Mindy safe while I take care of it."

Hayley reached up and clasped his wrist with her hand. Her skin was warm and her grip strong. She really was doing better.

She whispered, "What if it's more than just Mindy and me that need rescuing?"

The thought had been darting around in the back of his mind, but he'd been too overwhelmed to entertain it. Now, she'd laid it at his feet where it couldn't be ignored. The size of that lab, the number of people in it, hinted at a much larger operation. Rom doubted that Hayley and Mindy were the only test subjects.

"Anyone who's here not of their own will gets a pass," Rom said. "I'll do my best to protect them and get them to safety. However, you're my priority."

Mindy let out a long whining groan and pawed at him. He laughed, taking his hand away from Hayley's face so that he could pet the dog.

"And you, too," Rom said.

"Think I can get on that VIP list?" A feminine voice broke into the moment.

Hayley's eyes went wide and she sat up, forcing Rom to shift away a bit. She looked back at him, her mouth open as she stammered, trying to find something to say.

"Relax," the voice said. "I've looped the feeds so that it looks like you two lovebirds are still snuggling up in bed. Big Blue gave me a perfect in by telling you to rest. Norem thinks you're sleeping and has one of his goons on the monitors while he works on his *research*. I'd say you have a couple hours of privacy at least."

"Hayley, would you mind telling me who my new

second favorite person is?" Rom said.

Mindy grunted again and pawed at him.

"Sorry," he said. "Third."

The woman laughed and said, "She'd never out me. I can practically see the wheels turning in her head as she tries to come up with a cover for me. Don't worry, bestie, this is my decision. My name is Katie, and I think it's past time for us to blow this dump."

Chapter Seven

"I'm not sure I understand all of this vernacular," Rom said. "But I'm fine with blowing this place up after we leave."

Hayley couldn't believe that Katie was putting herself out there like this. She had been so careful not to let anyone know the extent of what she could do. Norem had seen Katie activate different controls and systems—always pretending that it was an unbearably difficult feat that she could barely manage—but she had kept the extent of her abilities secret. Even though Rom didn't know how Katie was manipulating the station's systems, the fact that she was letting him know that she could was a huge risk.

They knew so little about Rom. Or... did they?

"Katie, are you sure about this?" Hayley didn't dare ask a more pointed question, not wanting to give more things away that Katie didn't want to share.

"Oh yeah," Katie said. "This guy is our best bet for getting out of here. I'm putting my faith in you, Big Blue."

Rom arched an eyebrow at Hayley. "I'll do my best to live up to it."

"It shouldn't be too hard." Katie let out a laugh. "My god, is this serious?"

Hayley was used to having strange conversations with Katie where her friend commented on information Hayley didn't have. Rom was the unknown variable, and he was confused enough already. She sat up more, grateful when Rom pushed himself up to sit behind her so that she could lean against his chest. The aches in her back disappeared within moments. Whatever was causing his effect on her, she couldn't get enough of it. She hadn't felt so awake and energized in... She couldn't remember how long it had been.

"Did you find something useful?" Hayley asked her question using purposefully vague words.

"I'd say *you* did," Katie said. "According to the files, Rom is a Cygnian warrior."

Cygnian?

Hayley's stomach felt as if it was flooded with ice. When she had first been imprisoned with Norem, a Tau Ceti soldier named Tobek had come to Hayley and warned her that Sophie, Amy, Becca, Buddy—all of the Myers family—were in danger. They had been targeted by Dean. That was why the shapeshifter had come after Hayley. He wanted to use Hayley to be able to spy on them because Buddy had become friends with the Cygnian's crown prince.

By then, Haley had already seen enough to believe

Tobek and offered to get herself sent to Norem's research base to try to track down someone that Tobek had befriended and Norem had transferred—someone Hayley hadn't been able to find. Hayley hadn't really thought about the fact that she would be sent as one of Norem's test subjects. All she had been thinking about was keeping her family of the heart safe. Now, one of the aliens who had started this entire ordeal had found her. He was comforting her. Was it real or just another ruse? She had thought Dean cared about her and it had landed her in a nightmare.

Stupidly, for the first few... weeks? months? of her capture, she had dreamed about Dean coming to her rescue. She had heard enough from Norem and the other scientists and soldiers to know that they were afraid of Dean finding them. Taking her had angered him. Norem talked about it as if he'd stolen the Scorpiian's property.

Was that all Hayley had ever been to Dean? It didn't matter anymore. Her feelings for him were gone. She had to focus on the present moment, on getting herself and her friends out of here.

"They're from the planet Cygnus-Prime, which is located right next to a black hole," Katie continued doling out information, oblivious to Hayley's inner turmoil. "Their planet has a kind of crystal shell around it that protects them from most of the gravitational pull and radiation. Despite its protection, to survive, they've evolved to be almost indestructible."

"Indestructible." She could feel Rom nodding behind her. "I can work with that."

"You also have super advanced technology," Katie said.

Rom scoffed. "I don't even have a shirt."

"See those super sparkly wristbands?" Katie asked. "They're not just for show. Apparently, you activate them by smacking them together and then humming different control notes."

"I don't just push the buttons?" Rom lifted one arm to look at his wristband more carefully, turning his wrist back and forth. All Hayley saw was uniform, shiny chrome metal.

"What buttons?" Hayley and Katie asked at the same time.

"It's covered with lights in different shapes and colors." Rom held his arm closer. "See?"

"I don't see anything but the metal," Hayley said.

"He can probably see wavelengths the rest of us can't," Katie suggested. "It would make sense with all this data about spectrums, crystals, and wavelengths. These guys are all about light and vibration."

Hayley blushed as she could practically hear Katie's eyebrows wiggling through the feed. Even with Hayley's doubts, she couldn't deny the attraction she felt to Rom. She'd never felt anything like it before.

"Do you know what tones I need to hum to make them work?" Rom asked.

"Sorry, Blue. No clue." Katie snickered. "Wow, I'm a poet."

"Katie, you shouldn't be digging this deep into their files," Hayley said. "If Norem catches you..."

"Relax," Katie said. "I don't even have to dig. They're making this too easy for me. Ever since Blue here arrived, there's a bunch of Norem's goons who have been going crazy looking through every scrap of data they have on the Cygnians. All I have to do is sit back and watch the feed scroll by."

"I don't want you risking yourself," Rom said. "You should get back to wherever they're keeping you so that we can rescue you."

"I am where they're keeping me." Katie paused for a few moments. Hayley held her breath, waiting to see how much her friend was willing to share. She let it out as Katie continued. "I'm another one of Norem's science projects. I can connect with technology remotely."

"They give you access to a communications relay?" Rom's voice was heavy with skepticism.

"I don't need permission," Katie said. "If I'm close enough, I can pick the wavelengths out of the air. Let me actually get my hands on the tech and there's no stopping me."

"That's incredible," Rom said. His arms slid around

Hayley, pulling her closer. "I hate to ask, but I need to know what we're working with if we're going to make it out of here."

"I was supposed to be some kind of telepath." Hayley forced herself not to look at Mindy, even though she heard the dog whine. "It didn't work."

"I'm not so sure about that," Katie said.

When the line stayed silent, Hayley prompted, "You can't just say that and leave me hanging."

"I'm parsing through a lot of data here," Katie said. "Give me a minute."

What had Katie discovered? Did Norem know more about Hayley's ability to communicate with Mindy than Hayley knew? She remembered telling him that she could sense the dog's mind, but nothing about how intelligent Mindy was. It had still been enough for Hayley to draw Norem's interest.

"Norem thinks you're the reason Big Blue is here," Katie said. "He thinks he was drawn to you through some kind of... teleportation device?" Katie snickered. "Okay, this is just getting ridiculous. Unbelievable."

"We are being held captive and experimented on by vampire space frogs," Hayley said. "I think we're past dismissing the ridiculous."

"Okay, point taken," Katie said. "Norem just updated his personal files. He's so excited, he didn't even bother with any encryption. He says that he thinks Rom sensed you through blue space—hey, Big Blue, it's like natural camouflage for you."

"Katie." Hayley couldn't keep the impatience from her voice.

"Sorry," Katie said. "Anyway, Norem thinks Rom was drawn to you and that's why he appeared in your cell."

"So, Norem's largest experiment worked?" Hayley said. "Am I telepathic now?"

"No." Katie paused for dramatic effect. "You're Rom's soulmate."

Hayley wanted to laugh, but Rom stiffened behind her. His arms tightened, pulling her closer against his chest as if she was the most valuable treasure in the universe. She leaned to the side so that she could look up at him. His violet eyes had started glowing again and she was certain that, if he weren't leaning against the headboard, his spine plates would be vibrating like crazy.

"You can't believe that," Hayley said.

Rom's eyes sparked even brighter.

"Katie," he said, "I need you to check through all the records you can and find out if there are any other prisoners being held here. After that, we need a way out. Routes, patrol schedules, and most of all a ship. I'll be the muscle, but I need information if I'm going to keep you all safe. That starts with how you get the info. No unnecessary risks. Got it?"

"Ooo, I do love a man who can give orders," Katie

said.

"One more, then," Rom said, still holding Hayley's gaze with an intensity that had her toes curling. "I need you to give us some privacy for the next little while."

There was a pause before Katie said, "Hayley, are you okay with that?"

"Yeah," Hayley said, surprised to realize she meant it.

"Alright, then." Katie laughed. "You kids have fun. I'm signing off."

There was a beep, then silence. Hayley knew that Katie would give them the privacy they asked for. What she didn't know was why she wanted it so badly.

"*He completes you,*" Mindy thought.

"*I don't need anyone to complete me.*"

"*Not like that.*" Mindy let out a frustrated huff, lifting her face to stare into Hayley's eyes.

Hayley lifted her chin defiantly. "*I'm not missing anything.*"

The moment the thought entered her mind, another image flashed alongside it. She was back in the tank, watching Norem talk to himself—literally. Why did she keep remembering two of him? Wasn't one bad enough? They were passing off that cylinder again. Hayley had no idea why it was so important. She tried to look more closely, to see what it was, even as dread pooled in her stomach. Mindy let out a loud whine, bringing Hayley's attention back to the room.

"Are you okay?" Rom asked.

"Yeah. Yeah, I'm fine." Maybe if she said it enough, it would be true.

Mindy rose and leapt down from the bed, heading toward the bathroom.

"Now, where is she off to?" Rom mused.

"I think she's trying to give us privacy, too."

Rom chuckled. "That's very kind of you."

Hayley's heart gave a little stutter as she realized he was talking to Mindy directly. She didn't think he'd picked up on their secret, but he did seem to extend more respect to Mindy than anyone else Hayley had seen interact with the dog. It warmed Hayley's heart to see him treating Mindy so well. Mindy paused and looked back at them briefly.

"You can be whole within yourself and still be missing something," Mindy thought. Then she turned and trotted into the other room. A moment later, the door slid shut behind her.

"That dog is as sweet as she is smart," Rom said.

"You have no idea."

Now that they were alone, Hayley's nerves started to tingle. Part of it was that she was basically lying on a gorgeous blue alien who wasn't wearing anything from the waist up. In her fantasies, she'd be all over this guy. She would take charge and tell him what to do and he would respond as if instinctively knowing exactly what she liked.

But that was fantasy. This was reality. And in reality, she was aware that most of her nervousness came from the realization that she had only just met this man—this *alien* —and she already trusted him more than just about anyone she'd ever met. The intensity of it as well as the speed made her not trust… trusting him.

Sophie had told Hayley to go for it with Dean, and Hayley had listened. For once, she'd decided to take the leap, and it had landed her in Norem's clutches. But if she hadn't been willing to explore things with Dean, she wouldn't have had this chance to help Mindy and Katie and anyone else wanting to escape this hellhole. Her family of the heart was safer because of actions Hayley had taken since landing on Norem's radar.

Hayley couldn't go back and change the past. She wasn't even certain she would if she could. But she could make better decisions in the future. She could listen to her gut this time. Only this time, her gut wasn't telling her that something was wrong. It was telling her that something was right. That *everything* was right.

'*You are my everything.*' Rom had sounded so earnest when he said that. Hayley believed him, even though she knew she probably shouldn't. Even though it sparked the most dangerous thought of all within herself—one that felt so right, she couldn't reason herself out of believing it.

He's my everything, too.

Chapter Eight

"I need to talk to you," Rom said. "But I have to be able to see your face when I do."

"I can sit up." Hayley started to lean forward, but Rom tightened his arms around her.

"No way, sweetheart."

There was no way he was letting her weaken herself further. Not when she had only just started to look like she was feeling okay. That waxy, colorless cast to her skin had scared the crap out of him. He had thought he might be losing her, had even felt her slipping away. The more he held her, the better she seemed, the stronger. He wouldn't risk her backsliding.

Hayley leaned to the side so she could arch an eyebrow at him. "Katie might like the orders, but I'm not that kind of girl."

Rom grinned. "I believe it. Any other time, I'd do anything you say." His voice dropped as his smile faded. He cupped her face with his hand, amazed at how small and fragile she seemed. "Right now, I have to know you're okay. Please, just let me take care of you."

Her lips parted slightly, her cheeks getting that beautiful blush. It spread down her neck and over her collarbones, drawing his gaze lower—to places he had no business looking at or even thinking about. At the same time, it was hard not to, with her sleight weight on his chest.

As gently as he could, he lifted her and turned her around to face him, sitting up and crossing his legs. He deposited her in the little nest that position created, with her legs draped over his thigh. He cradled her back with one arm and used the other to gently trace the line of her cheekbone.

Her features were so delicate, huge blue eyes, lush lips that finally held a healthy pink to them. He longed to bury his fingers in her bright red hair, to pull her close and kiss her until all the nightmares of this place were forgotten. Instead, he lifted one of her hands and then the other, placing them above his hearts. Her eyes widened as she felt their strong, discordant beats.

"You have two hearts?"

"I do," Rom said. "I know that when I touch you, you feel better."

She blushed and looked away, but then nodded. Her hands stayed firmly pressed to his chest, his hearts beating faster beneath them.

"There's no shame in it," he said, lifting her chin with one finger. "I'm grateful that I'm able to bring you ease.

But you should know, it's not one-sided."

The faintest crease appeared between her eyebrows. "What do you mean?"

Rom gingerly placed his hand above her heart, curling his fingers over her collarbone. Her own heartbeat picked up, but then steadied and slowed a bit. As it did, his hearts followed suit, their beats becoming closer and closer to a single, strong beat.

"You can feel that, can't you?" Rom said. "How being close to you, touching you, affects me, too? I couldn't explain it before, but then your friend told us what was in that file. About us being soulmates."

Hayley shook her head. Her hands dropped away from him to fall into her lap.

"Don't dismiss it," Rom said. "Please."

"You don't even know who you are." Hayley's voice was barely above a whisper. Rom strained to hear her. "You didn't know *what* you are. How can you know that it's true?"

"There are things I know are true when I hear them," Rom said. "Like my name. Like being a Cygnian warrior. But I didn't need to hear your name to know you. I already knew you. I felt you. However I made my way to you, I believe the file is right. It's because you hold the other part of me. The other half of my soul."

"It could be something Norem put in the file just in case someone accessed it. It could be a trick."

Hayley refused to meet his eyes. A tear escaped one, rolling down her cheek. Rom reached out and smoothed it from her skin with the back of his fingers.

"I think you're afraid to let yourself believe it's true," Rom said. "You've lost so much already. Had so much taken from you. In any case, I believe you feel it the same way that I do. The echoes of my emotions. The rightness of us being close."

His voice dropped low as his throat tightened with emotion. What if he was wrong? What if she was right and this was a trick? Rom didn't doubt Norem would stoop to something as sadistic as making them think they were part of each other. That they were made for each other. Deep down, Rom couldn't believe this was a trick. It felt too real. At least, it did for him.

"Tell me you feel it, too," he said.

She finally met his eyes, her lips parting as she reached up and slid her fingers through his hair. Rom's hearts started to race, their pounding beat almost making him dizzy. She drew him closer, till their mouths were only a breath apart.

"I do," she whispered softly.

Rom's chest felt as though it was about to explode. He couldn't breathe, didn't dare to move. Time seemed to stop... until she pressed her lips against his.

She was tentative at first, her lips cautiously exploring his. Rom held himself still, letting her take the lead. His hands ached to pull her closer, his dicks straining against his pants. He wanted more. More closeness. More skin touching skin. But more than anything, he wanted not to scare her off.

She gripped his shoulders and pulled herself up so that she was straddling him. His control almost snapped. Whether she was struggling with her own or could sense his need and took mercy on him, she deepened the kiss at last, flicking her tongue across his lips. He opened to her immediately, welcoming her more intimate explorations, languidly stroking her tongue with his.

Her skin was so soft. He was almost afraid his stubble might abrade her. It didn't stop her from shifting her lips to his jaw, nibbling along it till she made her way to his ear and nipped at his earlobe. Pleasure arced along his nerves, lighting up every cell in his body. He was hyper aware of her arms wrapped around his neck, her warm breath against his skin, her small breasts pressed firmly against his chest.

"Rom," she murmured into his ear. Shivers spread over his skin at the sound of his name in her voice.

"Tell me," he whispered. "Tell me what you want and it's yours."

She leaned back so that she could stare into his eyes, a soft smile playing at her lips. "I want you."

His hearts were racing, beating against his chest. His breath went deeper, the rush of air making him feel more alive than he ever had before. He buried his fingers in her hair. The fiery strands were silken, softer than he'd imagined. He pulled her close for a passionate kiss, his tongue plunging into her mouth, staking his claim. She matched every thrust, her fingernails raking across his back as she pressed her core against his erections.

More ecstasy crashed through him. He reached down to grip her hips, grinding against her, wanting desperately to bury himself in her heat. Still, he held himself back, not wanting to hurt her nor frighten her in any way. This needed to be healing for both of them, this experience of union, of... unity.

Unity...

Her hands left his back, shifting between them so that she could unzip her jumpsuit. He helped tug it down her arms, freeing them from the drab garment. She broke off the kiss just long enough to pull the plain white sports bra she wore over her head and toss it aside. Rom didn't miss the opportunity to worship her breasts. He ducked his head to first one, then the other, pulling each tight bud between his teeth and flicking it with his tongue.

Hayley groaned, her fingers buried in his hair, holding him tight as she rocked against his dicks. He gripped her hips and lifted her so that she could stand. Her knees wobbled, but she kept her balance on the soft mattress. Rom still looked up at her with concern.

"I'm fine," she said, her voice breathless. "Better than

fine."

"Thank the Maker."

Rom grabbed her jumpsuit and panties at once and tugged them down her legs. She leaned on his shoulders for balance as she stepped out of them, awkwardly shimmying out of her boots as well so he could toss them aside. When she was fully naked, she started to lower herself to him again, but he gripped her waist and held her up. Her brow furrowed again as she cast a questioning glance his way, but he merely grinned in response. Then he leaned forward and buried his face in the soft curls between her legs.

Hayley gasped, her hands once more going to his hair. She groaned as he flicked his tongue across the small pearl buried in her silken folds. He slid one hand around to cup her backside, pressing her more firmly against his mouth. The other went to her core, gathering her wetness before sliding two fingers deep within her. Her grip tightened on his hair, her hips rocking against him.

He spread his fingers, working them in and out, massaging her channel and helping to prepare her for him. Her sex clenched his fingers, her breathing becoming more rapid. She would fall into ecstasy any moment. Her body stiffened and then she pushed against him suddenly.

"Wait," she said.

Rom quickly released her, staring up with worried eyes. Had he hurt her? Was she having a relapse? Or had she changed her mind? Of the three, his preference would be for it to be the latter. He would rather take on the agony of her rejection rather than have her be in pain again. When he looked up at her, she didn't seem angry or afraid. He opened his hearts to her, trying to pick up her emotions.

Warmth. Desire. Affection. He couldn't tell if they were coming from him or her or both of them.

"I want it to be with you," she said.

He let out a huge breath, relief washing through him. She smiled and pushed his shoulders to get him to lie back, then dropped down to straddle him again. He helped her undo his pants, finally freeing his erections. The cool air against his heated skin sent more shivers over his skin. He glanced up to see her staring at his dicks with huge eyes.

"What's wrong?" he asked.

She swallowed hard. "It's just... There are two of them."

"Yeah. Is that not... normal?"

She shook her head. "Not where I'm from. And they're not usually that big."

"I don't want to hurt you," he said, starting to lift himself onto his elbows.

She pushed him back down. "I'm sure we can work this out. Just... one at a time."

"Whatever you need, sweetheart."

With a smile, she bent over him once more. She captured his lips more boldly this time, lowering her hips to his so that his bottom dick lined up with her slit. Slowly, she drew herself along its length, so warm and wet. Rom thought he would lose his mind if he couldn't bury himself in her soon. His prayers were answered when she pressed her core to his crown and inched down, her body spreading as it welcomed him.

He kept himself as still as he could, giving her complete control so that he wouldn't hurt her by going too quickly. It took all of his self-restraint not to thrust himself into her. His hands shook as they trailed down the smooth skin of her back. Hayley placed her hands against his chest and lifted herself up on her knees so that she straddled him again. The movement pressed him deeper, and he let out a groan. She smiled at him softly, her eyes heavy-lidded.

She rose up on her knees, then lowered herself back down over and over, each time, taking him further into her slick heat. Electricity fired along his nerves, his skin alive with it. He had never felt such torment nor such pleasure. Finally, she slid down, taking him fully within her. Her sex was already starting to pulse as his upper dick nestled against her clit.

"Hayley…" Her name was both a moan and a plea.

She nodded and said, "I'm ready."

"Thank the Maker."

Rom gripped her hips and thrust up into her welcoming sheath with long quick strokes that kept her gasping. Pressure built within him, heat burning through his body, radiating out from where they were joined. He felt her tense, then she cried out, her fingernails raking across his chest. He increased his pace, coaxing as much pleasure from her as he could as he found his own release.

Nothing could ever feel this good. It didn't seem possible. And yet, even without his memory, he knew they weren't done. His upper dick throbbed, anticipating its turn at being buried within her. He pulled her against his chest, letting her catch her breath for a moment. Every instinct told him to thrust into her again. But he needed her to be ready. Ready for something he didn't truly understand, but that called to him, to his soul.

Unity...

Chapter Nine

How could Hayley feel utterly relaxed and yet amped up at the same time? Her body was tingling everywhere, a strange anticipation building within her. She'd just had the best climax of her life and usually only wanted to take a nap after. This time, she wanted to line herself up with that second fully-ready dick and go to town—again. The fatigue that had been plaguing her retreated, along with the aches and pains. She couldn't explain it, except that it was like stretching when she was super stiff and sore and feeling the tension release all at once on a cellular level.

I have definitely been in a mad scientist's sci-fi lab for too long.

The thought sent an unpleasant shiver down her spine. Rom immediately tensed, running his hand over her back as if chasing the feeling away. Miraculously, it vanished beneath his touch.

"What's wrong?" he asked.

"Just thinking about things that I really don't want to think about." She ran her fingertips along his cheekbone, then over his jaw. "Help me clear my mind? Just for a little while longer?"

Rom reached up and clasped her hand, bringing it to his lips to kiss her palm. He pressed it against his face, his eyes closing. When they opened again, their glow had intensified.

"Anything for you," he said.

In a different scenario, she would be a little worried about how devoted he was, but in this nightmare, he was a beacon of light. It wasn't just because he was her best chance for escape. He gave her hope that there was something for her to escape to. A future with the two of them together—with Mindy as well. They would all return to Earth and live in her family home. She'd introduce Katie to her chosen family and they would welcome her just as they had Hayley. It would be perfect. Just as it was this moment, lying in his arms.

Rom rolled her onto her back, lining up the dick that was still rock hard. He brushed her hair away from her face, staring at her as if memorizing her features. Then he kissed her deeply, passionately. He pulled back and stared into her eyes.

"I am yours," he said.

Her throat tightened with emotion. He hadn't claimed her. He had offered himself. After everything she'd been through, that one gesture of kindness nearly undid her. Everything he'd said before was right as well. She felt it in her bones, in her... In her soul. She smiled and nodded up at him.

"I'm yours, too," she said.

He let out a breath, his entire body relaxing. Well, not his *entire* body. She could feel him poised at her entrance, waiting to ensure she was truly ready.

"It's okay," she said. "You don't have to hold back." His brow furrowed, so she reassured him further. "I want all of you. I... I need you. Everything you can give me. I can handle it."

He lowered his head, his body shuddering as he quickly slid into her. Her sheath stretched to accommodate him, sending white-hot arcs of pleasure along her nerves. How could she be so worked up again already? Her heart pounded in her ears, her skin rose in goosebumps everywhere. Her inner heat built as he thrust into her, over and over again. He landed harder, his strokes becoming faster, stoking a fire within her that felt as though it would consume her. She wanted it to. She wanted to be remade into something that was *hers*. Something that was his as well.

The thought unsettled her, but only for a moment. Then Rom was kissing her, as if he could sense her turmoil. His tongue branded her mouth, all the passion he'd held back before pouring into her.

He held himself up with one elbow so that he could reach up with his other hand and cup her breast, pinching and rolling her nipple between his finger and thumb. Her core clenched, a pulsing beat picking up where they were joined. She clenched his shoulders, feeling his muscles flex beneath her hands. How could that be so erotic?

Electric heat built even higher within her, her nerves on fire, her body screaming for release. His hand slid down her side to her leg, lifting it and wrapping it around his waist, letting him land harder and reach even deeper within her. A wave of ecstasy hit her, her body lighting up with an energy she'd never felt before.

Rom's dick answered the pulsing pull of her sex, urging him to his own release. Her vision whited out as she felt him spill himself within her, heard him cry out her name. Her body hummed as though it was a tuning fork that had been perfectly struck, every cell in her body vibrating with pleasure.

Beyond that, she felt... good. There was no pain anywhere. No aches. No bizarre feelings in her joints and limbs, as if they didn't know what they were doing or had never been connected before. Her mind was clear, her body felt... sturdy. Stable. She hadn't realized just how bad off she had been until this very moment. Her body finally felt like it *worked*.

Well, except for her vision. She blinked, trying to clear the white light from her eyes. She stared past Rom's back at the ceiling as it came into focus and gasped. Rainbows filled the space around them. Thousands of them. Somehow, they floated in midair, not being cast on anything but just... being.

"What am I seeing?" she asked, breathlessly.

Rom chuckled, sending more pleasant vibrations through her body from where they were still joined. He nuzzled her neck, then kissed it with a skill that had her toes curling. He made his way to her ear, sucking on her earlobe and ever-so-gently raking his teeth across it. Her core clenched again, and he let out a rumbling growl of approval. Something in his mannerism had changed. Not in a bad way, just... He was different.

He leaned up to stare into her eyes. His face was more relaxed, lines of strain she hadn't recognized before gone. There was a confidence to his manner that was new, too. He ran his nose along her neck so that he could murmur his words into her ear, his warm breath making goosebumps rise along her skin.

"That is unity, sweetheart," he said. "And you had better get used to it, because you're going to be seeing those rainbows a whole lot."

"What—"

Before she could finish her sentence, she felt him slide from her body, then immediately plunge into her with his second dick again. She gasped, arching her back as a fresh wave of pleasure cantered along her nerves. He released his grip on her leg, but only so he could use that hand to reach between them and swirl his thumb over her clit.

Another climax crashed through her, intense enough to

make her cry out. Her eyes clenched shut. He claimed her mouth again, his thrusts quickening, drawing out the incredible sensations spiraling out from where they were joined. When she managed to open her eyes again, the rainbows had multiplied and were swirling in little circles. Rom grunted, his dick pulsing with her. Maybe now they could talk about—

Nope, once more he slid from her and immediately filled her with his other dick. Holy crap, were they ever going to leave this bed again? She almost didn't mind, except there were people counting on her.

"Rom." The rest of her sentence was swallowed on a gasp as he pulled himself from her, then thrust back in.

"Yes, Hayley?" He grinned as he looked down at her, completely aware of the carnal carnival he was taking her body to.

She smiled, despite the seriousness of their situation, then gasped again as he angled his hips, hitting her in a particularly sensitive spot.

"You really…" Another gasp. "…know what you're doing here."

"I've learned everything I can to keep pleasing you in as many ways as you'd like," he said. "As often as you'd like."

"I can… I can see that. But we need to talk."

He nuzzled her neck, brushing her ear with his nose again and nibbling on her earlobe. "We're talking now."

She laughed. Her chest tingled, her lungs filling with energy. It felt as if she had never laughed before. She had thought she never would again, certainly not while she was still in this hell. But somehow, this extraordinary, gorgeous, alien man made her laugh, even here.

A playful energy emanated from him. It was more than his mannerisms. As contented as she was in that moment, she was far from being able to feel anything so free. Was she sensing his emotions?

Something deeper lay beneath his happiness. A warmth and affection that soaked into her with an intensity that brought tears to her eyes.

Soulmate stories had never really been Hayley's thing. She didn't like the idea of needing to be completed by someone else. There was something about this, something about being held in Rom's arms, about feeling him buried deep within her, that made her realize it wasn't about being complete or not. It was about connection. She had never felt more connected to anyone before. Not even Mindy when they spoke in each other's minds.

"I really hope Mindy can't hear us," Hayley whispered.

"I bet she's asleep in the other room," Rom murmured against her neck. "It's what Ed and Zorro would do, and they aren't half as smart as she is."

"Ed and Zorro?"

"A Newfoundland and a Saint Bernard. They belong to a couple of friends of mine in Harbor, Kansas."

"Wait…"

That level of detail was unexpected. Rom had said that he sensed when things people said were right, but he hadn't conjured up information like that before. As if he could sense her confusion, he pushed himself up onto his elbows to smile down at her with a cocky, lopsided smile.

"Unity happens when Cygnian soulmates claim each other for the first time—and every time after," he said. "Their souls connect in their bodies' union, letting their essences mingle and restoring their balance. You look like you're feeling a hell of a lot better."

"I am," she said, still staring up at him in awe.

"Me, too," he said. "So much so that I got my memory back."

Her eyes widened. "That's wonderful!"

"Mmm-hmm." He hummed against her neck, sending a delicious vibration through her body. As he did, he started moving again, leisurely thrusts that set her nerves simmering.

"Do we really have time for this though?" she said. "I mean, you have your memory back, so we should make a plan to escape."

"Or bide our time till the cavalry comes."

Her heart quickened. "What do you mean?"

"I mean I'm part of a prism." He shifted his hips, changing the angle of his thrusts and somehow stimulating her in new ways. The more he spoke, the faster her heart beat. "Seven Cygnian warriors with their own sort of soul bonds. The bonds of brotherhood. We can feel each other, no matter where we are. Which is why I know they're on the way here to help rescue every single person who needs rescuing and wreak vengeance on those who don't."

She hadn't dared to dream of that. All she had wanted was a chance to escape with Mindy and Katie. A shadow rose up within her as she pictured those who had tortured her facing the same torment. Rom paused his movements, lifting himself on his elbows so he could stare down into her eyes. He kissed her so tenderly that her heart ached. When he broke off the kiss, he left their foreheads touching.

"Let it go, Hayley," Rom whispered. "Just for now. We can put on the mantle of war when we're ready. For these few blessed moments, let's just be with each other. Let us heal."

Tears filled her eyes, but she blinked them away and smiled. The terrors she had faced were in the past. Now, in Rom's arms, she finally had the courage to dream of a brighter future.

Chapter Ten

He had found her. Rom could scarcely believe it. In all the infinite universe, he had found his soulmate. All it had taken was for him to leap through a transit portal without knowing if it would spit him out somewhere or blow him up. He couldn't believe he had traveled through blue space without a ship. Tarn and Nancy had made it through, but Rom hadn't been certain when he tried it himself. It had been a literal leap of faith. At the same time, it hadn't been optional.

He had sensed her. Sensed Hayley. He remembered now.

There was a flicker in his awareness, like kindling finally catching fire. He'd known in that instant that his soulmate was out there. Why he hadn't sensed her before was a mystery, but he had been certain she was out there and that she needed him. Little did he know just how much. He tightened his embrace, holding her more closely in his arms as she slept after several more rounds of unity.

Her coppery hair looked beautiful splayed across his blue skin. He ran his fingers through the silken strands, amazed at how soft they were. Then he traced her cheekbone with his fingertips as lightly as he could, wanting her to rest, but being unable to keep himself from touching her. She was so delicate, her skin luminous. She was a marvel, his own miracle.

The bloodless look she'd had earlier was gone. Her lips were pink. The lines of strain around her eyes had vanished, and she was breathing easier. Whatever had been wrong with her before seemed to have resolved itself. Rather, unity had resolved it, just as it had restored his own equilibrium and helped him retrieve his memories.

Norem and his goons were in for a shock when they tried something again. Among the memories Rom had recovered was the knowledge needed to use his wristbands. The Tau Ceti wouldn't stand a chance against Cygnian technology. As soon as Hayley woke up, he would give them to her and teach her how to use them to protect herself. He was pretty much invulnerable, so it made sense for her to wear them. If that meant he'd have to launch himself into battle and tear apart the people who had hurt her with his bare hands, so be it. He only wished he had a way to protect Mindy and Katie, too.

"You have a lot of thinky thoughts going on," Hayley murmured.

"I didn't mean to wake you."

"It's okay. I feel like I've been sleeping for ages, but this is the first time I feel rested."

Rom chuckled. "How rested?"

She smiled, then opened her eyes and looked up at him. Maker, she was so beautiful. He brushed a lock of hair behind her ear, memorizing every detail about her.

"As tempting as that is, we should probably start to plan our escape," Hayley said. She laughed lightly and added, "If you're done counting my freckles."

Rom's brow furrowed. He stroked the backs of his fingers over her cheek.

"You don't have any freckles," he said.

Hayley arched an eyebrow at him. "I have thousands of freckles, see?" She lifted her arm for him to view, but he didn't see anything. She must have noticed as well, because she sat up, staring at her arm intently. "This doesn't make sense."

"Maybe they faded while you've been on the station," Rom said.

"I don't know. My freckles have never faded completely. I mean, they get a bit paler in the winter when I don't get as much sun, but I've always still seen traces of them." She checked her other arm, running her fingers along her skin as if she might be able to feel what she couldn't see. "I used to have a mole here." She bent her legs and examined her knees, anxiety rising within her. "And I had scars on both my shins from a bad fall when I was a kid. They're all gone."

Rom sat up next to her, running his hand along her

back. The fear within her gave way to a deep void of despair. He pulled her against his chest, hugging her tight.

"What did he do to me?" she whispered.

"I don't know," he said. "But we'll find out. We'll get you answers."

"Guys?" Katie's voice came over the room's speakers. She paused for so long, Rom worried that something might have happened to her, but then she continued. "I think I can help with that. You might want to get dressed first."

Hayley glanced up at Rom, her eyes glittering with unshed tears. He was going to rip Norem limb from limb for making her cry. For everything he'd done to her, as well as to Katie and Mindy. Hayley slid from his arms and rose on steady legs. Rom was at least glad to see her doing so much better. He quickly rose and dressed—not that it took him long since all he had to wear was a pair of pants and boots.

He hurried to Hayley's side to help her shimmy into her jumpsuit. As she zipped it up, he found her boots and brought them to her. They both sat on the edge of the bed, as close as they could be to each other. Katie didn't speak again till Hayley had tugged on both boots. Rom wasn't sure if they were going to need to make a run for it or Katie was stalling, not wanting to tell them whatever she'd found. His stomach sank as he figured it was the latter reason.

"Did you find other prisoners?" Hayley asked at last.

"No," Katie said. "As far as I can tell, Mindy, you and I are the last ones left. And we aren't prisoners. We're test subjects."

Rom's hearts started racing, following Hayley's quickening beat. He wrapped his arm around her, trying to offer strength and comfort.

"But, there were others," Hayley said, glossing over Katie's pointed remark.

"Yeah." Katie paused for a long time again.

"What happened to them?" Rom finally prompted. He wanted to know just how merciless he needed to be with Norem.

"Norem has been accessing files that he's never looked at while I was watching him before," Katie said. "He thought he was keeping his data safe by storing it on a device separate from the station's servers, but I was able to change the angle of the security cameras so that I could read over his shoulder."

She was definitely stalling. Rom didn't want to push, knowing she had probably been through her own trauma at Norem's hands, but they didn't know how much time they had left before Norem came knocking on their door. It would take his prism time to reach them. They needed a plan for how to keep everyone safe until backup arrived. He needn't have worried, because Hayley was just as impatient as he was to learn more.

"And?" she said.

"The great news is that M-1 through M-36 are all living happy lives on Earth with loving families," Katie said.

Hayley let out a rush of breath. She pressed her hand against her chest, as if she was trying to keep her heart from leaping out from it. Rom covered her smaller hand with his and kissed the top of her head.

"I was always afraid that's what M-37 meant," Hayley said. "That there were others out there like Mindy."

"You were right about the others, but the 'out there' part is actually really nice," Katie said. "Norem has been visiting breeders on Earth for years and secretly injecting the dogs with genetically engineered cocktails in an attempt to heighten certain abilities. His reports didn't say what they were, but each generation made advancements. Mindy was the first subject that he considered a success, so Norem brought her to the base. He's still keeping track of the rest of her cousins, siblings, parents, and grandparents."

"Do you have the names and addresses where those other pups are?" Rom questioned. Hayley glanced up at him, so he explained. "Just because they didn't meet his standards doesn't mean that he didn't succeed in altering them. We need to make sure they get the care they need and that we can have our own people monitor them for possible health issues resulting from his tinkering."

Hayley turned her hand in his so that she could squeeze it. A wave of such love flowed out from her that he gasped from its intensity. He leaned forward, resting his forehead against hers again.

"There's more." Katie spoke hesitantly, as if she didn't want to break into their moment, but also couldn't let it go on.

"I take it from your tone that the 'more' isn't good," Hayley said.

"You know me well, bestie," Katie said. "Norem looked through your file." She pulled in a harsh enough breath that Rom could hear it over the comm channel. As far as he knew, she was holding it, because she stopped talking again.

"And?" Hayley said.

A few more seconds passed. Rom heard Katie let her breath out, then make a few incomprehensible noises. He was just about to prompt her again when she spoke.

"It was labeled H-7," Katie said.

Hayley looked up at Rom, her eyebrows furrowed. He could feel his own confusion mirrored in her. Why was that such a bad thing? Katie said it as if it was a death sentence. Then she went on, and Rom's hearts started thundering on their own.

"H-0 is still labeled as active." Katie's voice was low and soft. "But, um… H-1 through H-6 are listed as failed. As in… deceased."

"Wait, what?" Hayley shook her head. "Why would there be multiple files for one—"

Her eyes widened and her mouth fell open. She clapped her hand over it as if she was trying to hold back a cry. It did nothing to hide the way her soul called out. Rom heard her horror as clearly as if she had screamed through their bond.

"What is it?" He pulled her closer, scanning the room for threats instinctively.

"This doesn't change anything," Katie said, forcefully. "We're still getting out of here together and you're still my best friend. You're still *you*. Hayley..."

Hayley pinched her eyes shut tight, as if hearing her name in that moment caused her pain. Tears rolled down her cheeks.

"I'll give you two a moment," Katie said, her voice once again soft and gentle. "Just say my name when you're ready for me to come back into the conversation."

There was a beep, then the only sound was Hayley's soft sobs.

"What is going on?" Rom asked, bewildered. He thought back to how sick Hayley had seemed when he first encountered her and his stomach felt as though it was flooded with ice. Had she almost died? Was that why she was so upset? Except she had stabilized after they achieved unity. She was fine now. Wasn't she?

He struck his wristbands together gently so as not to disturb her, then hummed the note to activate their scanning function. A small, holographic image of Hayley appeared behind her. Her vitals were fine. Everything looked great. The scans couldn't find a single thing wrong with her. Rom let out a breath of relief, then dismissed the hologram. He rubbed Hayley's back, holding her close.

"Okay, you're not the first person Norem experimented on for this project," Rom said. "And the others… They didn't make it. That's horrible, and we'll make him pay for it. But you're okay. You're fine. Hayley—"

"I'm not Hayley," she nearly shouted, pulling away from him and hugging herself tightly. A chill shot down his spine. She believed what she was saying, but Rom still didn't understand it. Katie had tried to reassure her, telling her she was still her, whatever that meant. Rom was missing something. Something important. Hayley shook her head, then buried her face in her hands. Rom knelt in front of her, resting his hands on her knees.

"Please help me understand so I can help you," Rom said.

She shuddered and took a deep breath, then dropped her hands into her lap. She stared at the backs of her hands as if she'd never seen them before.

"My… my…" she stammered. "My freckles are gone. And so are my scars."

"Okay," Rom said. "So, Norem tweaked your body when he was trying to make you telepathic. Or it was a side effect."

She shook her head. "It's more than that. I remember

things. *Hayley's* experiences." She looked up at the ceiling, fresh tears rolling down her cheeks. "God, how did he give me her memories? How did he make me think I was her?"

"Hayley…"

This time, she didn't chastise him for using her name, but she let out a pained groan, as if the word hurt her.

"I don't understand what's going on," Rom said. He picked up her hands, holding them gently in his and rubbing his thumbs over them. "What did Norem do to you?"

Such pain twisted her features, it took Rom's breath away. He stared at her, trying to think through the all-consuming despair radiating out through their bond.

"He created me," she said.

Chapter Eleven

"I'm not real." Hayley's heart pounded painfully in her chest. She could barely breathe. Thoughts whirled through her mind so fast it made her dizzy.

"What do you mean you're not real?" Rom asked.

Concern flowed out from him. She could feel everything he felt through their bond. She clung to that, trying to calm the maelstrom of her own emotions. Rom needed to know the truth. She had to tell him. But saying it… Saying the words… She pinched her eyes shut, ignoring the tears that spilled out from them. Rom deserved to know.

"I'm a copy." Her voice dropped down to a whisper. "I'm a clone."

Rom didn't blink. He didn't flinch. The steady concern and… love flowing out from him didn't blip at all. Did he not understand what she was saying? How could it not faze him even a bit?

"Rom, I'm not Hayley," she repeated, her voice stronger as rage rose up within her. How could Norem have done this to her? To Hayley? God, all those people who hadn't made it. All those versions of Hayley. Hayley, who was *not* her.

"I'm a clone." Each time she repeated it, something in her hardened. Somehow, she was going to make Norem pay for what he had done. But first, she had to get through this moment with Rom.

He was still staring up at her, his brow pinched in worry, his hands gently holding hers. He wasn't repulsed or even angry, just eager to help. It was as if he was waiting for her to continue, to tell him what he should do. What more did she have to say?

Finally, he said, "Okay…" dragging out the word. Then he shrugged. "So what?"

Her breath poured out of her in a gasp. "How can you be so flippant about this?"

"I'm sorry," he said. "I can feel how much this bothers you, but I don't understand why it upsets you so much. I've met lots of clones. The crown prince of my people has a sister who's been cloned so many times…"

Finally, his own anger rose up in him. He bowed his head, his spine plates rising with a menacing vibration. She tried to pull her hands away, but he held on. It wasn't that she was afraid of him. She felt unworthy. Everything that had passed between them had been a lie. Her existence was a lie.

"Don't do that, please." Rom rose up on his knees, pulling her hands against his chest. "Don't pull away from me. Please, tell me what's tearing you up inside."

"I thought everything was finally better," she said. "I thought we would be rescued and I could have my own 'happily ever after.' But it's not mine. It's Hayley's."

"Hayley…"

She glared at him and he snapped his mouth shut. He blew out a breath and shook his head.

"What happened between us happened between *us*," he said. "This doesn't change anything."

She let out a mirthless laugh. "How can it not? I'm *not* Hayley. You were supposed to bond with her."

"Just because there's another Hayley running around out there doesn't mean you aren't you," Rom said. "And it sure as hell doesn't mean that I'm supposed to bond with her."

A sharp pain lanced through her heart at the thought of Rom sharing the connection they had forged with another. The weight of it forced the air from her lungs in a sob. Rom wrapped his arms around her, pulling her firmly against his chest. He held her while she cried until she felt hollowed out. All the while, he poured his love for her into their bond, trying to soothe the ache within her.

"I have bonded with you," he murmured against her hair. "Unity can only be achieved between soulmates. You are your own person. You have your own soul. I know it for a fact, because it's the other half of mine. I can feel it. If there's another person running around who looks a lot like you and has the same memories, good for them. But they have their own soul. They are fundamentally a different person."

Could he be right? She felt connected to him in a way she'd never felt with anyone before. Not even her telepathic link with Mindy could compare. Rom really did feel like the other half of her soul. But what did that mean for the original Hayley? For 'H-0,' as Norem designated her.

It was too much. Hayley couldn't bear to think of it. She clutched Rom's back, clinging to him as if he was her anchor in a stormy sea. All the while, he kept whispering reassurances in her ear, the words finally breaking through the wall of agonized thoughts roiling in her mind. He pulled back, cradling her head between his hands.

"It doesn't matter how you got here," he said. "The important thing is that you *are* here. You are you. *You* are the other half of my soul."

And then he kissed her. His lips were tender at first, gentle. Heat still flooded her at the touch. It burned away her worry, her fear. She might not understand who or even what she was, but she understood this. His touch. The way it made her feel. She was his soulmate, and that made her different from everyone else in the universe. That made her unique. It made her... herself.

She wished they had time for more, but too much was at stake for them to get distracted. It wasn't just her own safety on the line. Katie and Mindy needed her, too. Rom broke off the kiss, pressing his forehead to hers. She loved it when he did that.

"I need to tell you something," she said. "Something that didn't make sense until now."

Rom sat back on his heels, staring up at her intently. "I'm listening."

"I keep having these visions—memories, I think. I'm in the tank and I see Norem watching me." She felt Rom tense, but if she paused, she didn't think she'd be able to get through this, so she powered on. "Someone else comes up to him and hands him…" She shook her head sharply, not wanting to focus on what was inside the cylinder. "He hands him something. I pound on the glass, and I can see that my left arm is made out of metal."

Rom hissed in a breath, a wave of rage blowing out from him that would have made her gasp if she didn't feel just as much anger herself. It bolstered her, helping her to go on. That wasn't the important part. The important part was what she needed to say next.

"The other man was also Norem," she said. "I thought it was just a weird dream or hallucination, but I'm sure of it now. If I have Hayley's memories, I think this really happened. There are multiple Norems as well."

Rom bowed his head, giving her a clear view of his spine plates. They vibrated so quickly, they blurred. She could feel his rage building, his efforts to calm himself. She cupped his face in her hands and tilted it up so she could see the vibrant violet glow of his eyes. Muscles strained in his jaw as he ground his teeth together.

"I'm sorry," she said. "It seemed important you should know that stopping him might be harder than you think."

"It's not that," he said. "We also had just recently discovered that there are multiple Norems. We ran into another one right before I came for you."

"Then what's upsetting you so much?"

"Norem has a lot of projects going on," Rom said. "I'd guess he's made a clone of himself for each project and probably uploads all of their memories in some sort of repository for them to share amongst each other."

"He can do that?" If such a thing were possible, it would explain how she had Hayley's memories.

"Lots of species can do that." Rom rested his hands on her legs. "The Coalition took it farthest—and to the worst possible uses—but the technology is floating around everywhere. When we went to Earth, we uploaded all of the languages into our brains so that we could talk to whoever we encountered. There's cultural programming as well, but that's only as good as our research."

"You can program yourselves like robots?"

He flinched, his jaw muscles twitching again.

"What is it?" she asked.

"Norem probably used the same technology to imprint Hayley's memories onto you when you were created," Rom said. When she started to pull back again, he followed, wrapping his arms around her hips and pulling her closer again. "Listen to me. Every member of the Coalition of Planets is grown in a maturation chamber. They go through all their stages of development, from infancy all the way through adulthood in that chamber. When their bodies are ready, the Coalition's genetic engineers download a set of skills into them based on the function each person is slated for in their society."

"Oh my God," Hayley gasped. "That's awful."

"Every Sadirian you meet is their own person, though. They start having their own life experiences as soon as they emerge, and it shapes them into a unique individual, even if they have the same base programming."

"Still..."

"Things are changing," he said. "Their High Council has been destroyed and most of the people who still call themselves part of the Coalition have moved to the Sol system. Earth has had a profound effect on them. I wouldn't be surprised if they did away with maturation chambers as soon as their society stabilizes from all the recent changes. But they might keep some, and the people who are created that way are just as valid. Just as you are."

Maybe he was right. It was still a lot to process, but it didn't hurt as much to think about. She didn't have time to brood about it or try to figure out the nature of her existence, though. Too much was at stake. One last thing was niggling at her mind, though.

"If you already knew about the multiple-Norems, why did you get so upset when I mentioned them?" she asked.

He flinched again, then sighed. "Norem has a lot of things going on. He's been working on the transit portal I used to get here, trying to make it so Tau Ceti can go through it without being pulped. Another version of himself has been adding Cygnian DNA to his soldiers, trying to make them stronger so they can withstand the portal's effect and complete the trip through blue space in one piece. The Tau Ceti have a long history of genetic engineering as well."

He glanced away, dread stopping his words.

"What aren't you telling me?" she said.

He ran his hand through his hair, then shook his head. "The other thing Norem is known for is cybernetics. He... He's been experimenting on his Tau Ceti soldiers, replacing body parts with mechanical versions to enhance their performance. If Hayley had a metal arm in your memory, that means..."

His eyes pinched at the corners and he trailed off, unable to finish. He didn't need to.

Hayley didn't dare close her eyes. If she did, she knew what she'd see. The contents of the cylinder. The part of the original Hayley that they had removed to make her a cyborg. That they had probably used... to make herself.

Hayley shook her head, then looked up at the ceiling. She couldn't let this overwhelm her. She couldn't give in to the rage and the fear. It was time to act. Time to take Norem down. With Rom at her side, she was certain they could do it. They would hunt down every version of Norem, wipe him out of existence, and save the original Hayley while doing so. She looked back at Rom, resting one hand on his cheek.

"Cygnians are warriors," she said, with a question in her voice. When he nodded, she continued. "If I'm your soulmate, that means I have a Cygnian soul."

"It's true."

"Then I think it's time I went to war."

Chapter Twelve

Here was his woman, his soulmate, a warrior through and through. Rom felt the fierce surge of power within her, fueling her, spurring her to act. He shared it, reveled in it —the warrior's drive. Clasping her hand, he pulled her toward the door, stopping when he remembered that they needed to bring Mindy with them. It would be tricky to keep all of them safe, but he would make it happen.

"Mindy," he called out. "Come on, girl."

The door to the bathroom slid open. Mindy skulked out, her tail tight between her legs and her nose close to the floor. She was letting out a near-continuous whine, obviously terrified.

"Oh no," Hayley muttered.

"It's okay, sweetheart." Rom let go of Hayley's hand and dropped down close to the ground, squatting near the dog and inching closer. "We're not going to let anything happen to you."

Mindy's whining increased. She would only look at them from the corner of her eye.

"Mindy," Hayley said.

"*Is it true?*" The words were spoken in a sweet, soulful

feminine voice, trembling with emotion. Did Mindy's collar allow her to talk, the same way as the space kittens Rom knew back in the Sol system? If so, why hadn't she spoken until now? He didn't have a chance to ask before she spoke again, angling her body toward Hayley. *"I know I wasn't supposed to listen, but you were so upset, I couldn't help myself. Are you really not my Hayley?"*

Hayley pinched her lips shut, tears welling in her eyes once more. She wrapped her arms around her middle, fresh pain resurfacing and battering at Rom through their bond. He did his best to keep his voice level.

"Hey, now," Rom said. "Come here."

Mindy licked her lips nervously, but approached till she was close enough for Rom to bury his fingers in her soft fur. She butted her head against his shoulder and let out a breath, followed by another plaintive whine.

"I am still your Hayley." Hayley's voice sounded different somehow. Softer and more… intimate. *"If you still want me to be."*

Rom's hearts broke for her. For both of them. He didn't want Hayley to have to deal with any more hurt. Being rejected by Mindy would devastate her. He held his breath, waiting to see what the dog would do. Mindy sniffed the ground, then slowly approached Hayley, flopping on her side when she reached Hayley's feet and then rolling over to show her belly. Hayley dropped to her knees and wrapped her arms around Mindy's neck, hugging her as if she would never let her go. Rom scooted over to join them, resting one hand on Hayley's back and another on Mindy's side.

"You're the luckiest pup in the universe," Rom soothed. "You get to have two Hayleys be your best friend."

Mindy let out a little yip, then rolled back so that she could sit on her haunches. She sniffed at Hayley, nuzzling her hair and licking her cheek. The relief Hayley felt was dizzying. Rom shared it as well.

Mindy paused and started whining again. *"You feel the same, but what happened to the first Hayley? Is she okay?"*

"I don't know," Rom said. "But, we're going to find out. We won't stop trying till we save her."

Mindy's tail started to wag, thumping on the floor where she sat. She angled her head up and licked Rom's chin. Rom ruffled her fur, stroking her neck and back in what he hoped would be a soothing manner.

"Thank you," Mindy said.

"Of course."

"Wait…" Uncertainty pushed its way to the forefront of Hayley's emotions. "Can you hear her?"

"Sure, I can," Rom said.

Hayley's eyebrows rose, then furrowed as she looked at him with intense concentration.

"Can you hear me?" she said. Her voice had shifted to

that softer, more intimate level.

Wait… She hadn't moved her lips or opened her mouth. How had Rom heard her at all? He blinked a few times, trying to sort things out. Mindy's mouth fell open in a doggie smile.

"*He can hear us now,*" Mindy said. "*You're better this way. The same.*"

"I don't get it," Rom said. "Am I not supposed to hear her?"

"Rom…" Hayley reached out and clasped his wrist with her delicate hand. She pinched her lips shut, but he still heard her go on. "*Don't say the words out loud. Just think them. Imagine that you're talking to us and push the words toward us.*"

"Holy…" He shook himself, then did as she instructed, focusing on projecting his thoughts toward them. "*The telepathy experiment… It worked?*"

Hayley let out a laugh and nodded. "*It did. But only between Mindy and me. I don't know how, but I could already talk to her when we first met.*"

"*The bad man has been trying to find someone I could talk to for a long time.*" Mindy barked as she thought the words to them. "*When Hayley came, I could talk to her, even when she wasn't close. Then she went to sleep for a while and when she woke up she was so far away. Until new Hayley came. Then she was close again.*"

"*Can you feel her?*" Rom thought. "*The first Hayley*"

you met?"

Mindy's ears perked up and she glanced to the side as if she was seeing something through the wall. *"I can still feel her. She's so far away..."*

Rom couldn't stop himself from letting out a huge breath, along with laughter. He hugged Mindy closer, pulling Hayley into the embrace as well.

"If you can feel her, that means she's still out there," Rom thought. *"It means we can find her."*

"The universe is a big place," Hayley thought.

"It doesn't matter." Rom shook his head. *"Mindy has a bond with both of you. It's the same as the bond I share with the other Cygnian warriors in my prism. I can feel them, wherever they are in the universe, and they can feel me. It's how I know they're coming for us and how I know we're going to be able to find the other Hayley. But first, we have to get ourselves out of here."*

"Norem has no idea we can communicate this way," Hayley thought to them.

"We can use that to our advantage," Rom thought. *"We just have to be careful not to slip up. I think it's time we call Katie."*

Hayley nodded, then stood. Rom followed, as did Mindy.

"Katie, we're ready to get moving," Hayley said, her voice strong. They waited several moments, but Katie didn't reply. "Katie? Are you still there?"

Anxiety rose within her. Rom reached out and clasped Hayley's hand.

"Maybe she's not in a place where she can respond," Rom said.

Hayley tightened her grip on his hand. "Her technokinesis lets her communicate through the computers without speaking. It's similar to my telepathy, but with machines."

"Has she ever not responded before?" Rom asked.

Hayley nodded as a fresh wave of panic flowed out from her. "When Norem has her in the tank."

Rom's stomach sank. His mind flashed to thoughts of the tanks at Norem's base on Ceres and the poor souls they had rescued from within. Tobek and Merek had adapted to their new cybernetic limbs and the Cygnian DNA that had been grafted into their bodies, but Alek was still struggling with pain and seizures. He hadn't learned how to control his cybernetics and the interface had been damaged before he emerged from his tank.

The thought of Hayley or anyone else in tanks like that had Rom's spine plates rising again. He struck his wristbands together and hummed several commands. They would continue to accept his audio instructions at a low power mode until he turned them off. He could activate shielding, atmospheric controls, even weaponry at a moment's notice. However, it wasn't himself he needed to protect. His final note caused them to expand so that he could slide them off of his forearms.

"I need you to wear these," Rom said.

Hayley shook her head. "If Norem sees me wearing them, he'll know you figured out how to use them again and that you have your memories back."

"I think that ship has left the starport," Rom said. "Please, I need you to be safe."

"None of us will be safe until we've stopped Norem once and for all."

Rom nodded. "I get that. But we have to get out of this mess before we can stop him."

Her scowl deepened, before she finally lifted her arms, pushing the sleeves of her jumpsuit out of the way. He quickly slid the bands over her slender wrists. They shrank down to fit her snuggly.

"These are the notes for shielding and atmosphere." He hummed each note in turn.

"Can they shield others, or just me?"

His hearts warmed at her concern. Her desire to protect others was just as fierce as his.

"Shielding others is hard to master," he said. "I hate to admit, I never trained in it. But we'll ask Dorn to fix that as soon as we're back on Earth. He's an expert at it."

Hayley nodded, her lip quivering as another wave of dread flowed out from her.

"What is it?" he asked.

"I just… I was thinking about Sophie and the rest of

her family," Hayley said. "Wondering what they'll think of me."

"They'll love and accept you, just as I have." He shrugged. "Actually, maybe not *just* as I have, but you get my point."

She let out a brief burst of laughter, as he'd hoped she would. "I guess we'll sort that out later, too. Right now, we have to get to Katie."

Rom nodded his agreement. "Do you know the way to the lab?"

"Yeah." Her dread returned.

Part of him wanted to protect her from this. From returning to that horrible place and confronting what she'd been through. He knew she had the soul of a Cygnian warrior. To offer to let her stay behind would be an insult. He knew better than even to suggest it. Mindy, on the other hand... Her tail had dropped when they started talking about the lab, and she was whining softly again.

"*I want you to be close, but you don't have to go into the lab with us,*" Rom thought. "*We'll find a place nearby for you to hide.*"

"*I want to help,*" Mindy thought.

"*I know, sweetheart,*" Rom thought back. "*But if helping hurts you, we don't want that.*"

She bumped his hand with her nose and licked his fingers, then lowered her head.

"*He's right,*" Hayley thought. "*We don't know what*

we're going to face in the lab. There's a room right next door where we clean up after leaving the tank. Can you wait for us there? It would really help me."

Mindy perked up, her ears angling forward and her tail wagging a bit. "*It would help?*"

Hayley nodded. "*I need you to be safe.*"

"*I need you to be safe, too,*" Mindy thought. "*Both of you.*"

"*Don't you worry about us.*" Rom reach out and scratched behind her ears. "*We're going to be just fine.*" He looked up at Hayley and said out loud, "You ready for this?"

She took a deep breath and nodded. "I am."

Chapter Thirteen

Walking to the lab felt like a march along death row. The corridors stretched in front of her, elongating in her mind's eye, yet passing much too quickly. She had barely blinked and they were hugging Mindy and telling her to be safe while she hid in the bathroom next to the lab.

The fact that Rom hadn't suggested that Hayley hide as well was something she would never forget. She knew he was just as desperate for her to be safe as he was for Mindy, but Hayley could also feel his respect and admiration for her, his confidence in her abilities. He believed in her, and that helped her believe in herself.

Rom reached out and clasped Hayley's hand as they stood before the door to the lab. He didn't say anything, just stared down at her, waiting for her to take the lead. She took a deep breath, then stepped forward, triggering the door's proximity sensors. It opened with a soft whoosh that sent a shiver down her spine.

Norem was inside, silhouetted by the eerie yellow of the softly glowing liquid that filled the much-smaller-than-usual cylindrical tank behind him. He had a serene smile on his face, though he was surrounded by chaos. The other scientists scurried about, grabbing equipment and shoving it onto hovercarts or carefully placing samples in stasis cubes. Norem's smile widened when he saw them.

"I was wondering when you would join us," Norem said.

He stepped aside so that they could see Katie floating in the small tank. It was only a few inches larger in diameter than her body. She would barely have room to move in it. A few strips of fabric were her only source of modesty and a crude mask covered the bottom half of her face. Her red hair floated around her in the liquid. Her eyes were open, pinched at the corners with fear. She shook her head when she saw them, bubbles escaping from the edges of her mask.

"Please tell me you were never treated like this," Rom thought to her, a sickening dread flowing through their bond to accompany the telepathic message.

Hayley didn't respond. She couldn't. Her heart pounded and her stomach churned. She felt as though she might throw up. She had been in that tank, or one just like it, too many times—she and the original Hayley. And even though most of the memories flooding her mind weren't her own, they felt as though they were. They felt real. Hayley knew the hell that Katie was experiencing. She had to save her from it.

Norem followed her line of sight to Katie and made a tutting noise. "I know it's not as comfortable as what you're used to. We had to go with a much smaller design —for ease of portability—and we're keeping everything as manual as possible with K-0 for now. She's saturated with neuro-suppressants, but it's best not to take chances. Now that I know just how successful my experiment with K-0 turned out, I can't have her playing with any doodads that manage to get too close." He turned back to them and gestured toward the tank with a small device he held in one hand. "Except for this one, of course. But she's already figured out that she doesn't want to activate it." He smiled, then pressed his thumb on the device.

Electricity crackled through the tank. Katie's eyes pinched shut, her body jerking. Hayley ran forward, but Norem made a point of pressing harder. Katie let out a pained scream that not even the liquid and the mask could fully muffle. Rom grabbed Hayley's arm and held her back.

"*We can't,*" Rom thought.

"Well done, Cygnian." Norem finally removed his thumb, though he kept it poised over the device. Katie went limp in the tank, floating in the water with her head listing against her shoulder. "K-0 already knows what your blue friend here has figured out. If this device is disabled or destroyed, it'll send enough voltage through her to kill her. I'd hate to see that happen, since I still need to study her brain and how it integrated so uniquely with the cybernetic components I implanted. She was supposed to be a blueprint for a new design of cybernetic controls to make my soldiers better at controlling their mechanical parts. It's truly exceptional work on my part."

Hate unlike anything Hayley had ever felt flooded through her. She would destroy Norem and everything he cherished. She would make him suffer the way he made others suffer. But how could she do that when he could torture her friend at the touch of a button?

"You kill her and you'll follow right after," Rom growled.

Norem shrugged. "Probably."

Rom was seething, rage and despair flowing out from him through their bond. The rage, she understood. The despair worried her, as did Norem's nonchalant response to knowing how close he was to death.

"You've already uploaded your recent memories into your master repository," Rom said.

"You *are* smart—for a Cygnian," Norem said. "It gives me hope that you'll understand what I'm going to say next. We're going to do a quick scan of H-7 before we leave."

"Leave?" Rom said.

"What, did you think I was going to hang around here and wait for your prism to find you?" Norem said.

Hayley's stomach sank. If Norem knew about the prism being able to track each other through their bond, he would keep them on the move. If so, could Rom's friends actually find them? Or would they always be just out of reach of help?

"Let's make sure we're all on the same page here." Norem leaned against a nearby table, crossing his hands in front of his body, the control device tauntingly out of reach. "You've figured out that I'm a clone—one of many, many clones, actually. I've recently uploaded my memories, so destroying me wouldn't really be much of a loss."

"That doesn't mean it won't be satisfying as hell to kill him," Rom thought.

Hayley didn't know if she could ever actually kill someone, but if she could, it would certainly be Norem. After what he had done to the original Hayley and everyone else, Hayley would at least enjoy watching Rom rip him apart.

"I know all about Cygnian prism bonds and how they can be used to track each other. It's not as powerful or effective as tracking through a soulmate bond, but I'm guessing it'd be enough to get them here. Hence, my summoning of a ship for us to relocate our operations."

He looked at her wrists pointedly. "I can see Rom's memories have returned. It was only a matter of time, so I'm glad we can get this all out of the way. I'll be taking those wristbands."

"Like hell," Rom said, taking a step forward.

Norem casually brushed his thumb across the device.

Katie's forehead furrowed, her head flying back as she convulsed again. Rom froze, shock and rage storming out from him. Norem lifted his free hand and waved his fingers, shooing Rom farther away. Spine plates up and vibrating violently, Rom took a step back. Norem released his grip on the device and Katie fell limp again.

"Please stop hurting her," Hayley said. "We'll do anything you say."

"How kind of you to say so." Norem smiled beatifically. "I'm sure you understand that I'm going to need you to keep your distance, though. I'd love to be able to trust you, but we're not quite there yet."

"*What do we do?*" Hayley thought.

"*I don't know.*" Rom's turmoil matched hers, amplifying her anxiety. He shook his head and glanced at her.

"Alright, now that is interesting," Norem said, standing straight again and pointing between Rom and Hayley. "I know that soulmates can feel each other's emotions, but that little exchange was something more."

Hayley's stomach sank. Dread and regret flooded Rom.

"*I'm so sorry,*" he thought, pointedly not looking at her.

"Oh, please," Norem said. "The cat's already out of the bag, as they say on Earth. Remember, I designed the H-series to be telepathic. The other prototypes didn't work out as expected, but you, my dear... You are delightfully intact." He looked at Rom. "I wonder what your part in that is. All of the other H-series lost cellular integrity within a day or two—a terrible, messy affair. I had actually run out of original base material for new clones. Luckily, I don't think that will be a problem anymore." Norem's attention returned to Hayley, a predatory gleam in his eyes. "You seem to have stabilized sufficiently to help me with a new supply of material."

"He can't mean..." Rom began.

The memory of the cylinder replayed in her mind. The object floating in the murky liquid. She tried to shut it off, to stop thinking about it, but after what Norem had said, realizing what he planned for her, knowing that the memory she had been given was a glimpse of her own future... She couldn't stop picturing it. Unfortunately, the image was so strong that Rom saw it, too.

"What the hell is that?" Rom thought. *"Did that happen to you? Did he do that to you?"*

"Not me," Hayley thought. *"The other Hayley. The original. They turned her into a cyborg. I guess... I think they used what they removed to make me."*

Shock tore through him, followed quickly by fury. *"I'll destroy the whole station before I let him touch you again. I will hunt down every single Norem in existence, everyone even related to him, and end each and every one of them."*

"We have to stay calm," she thought, though her stomach was churning.

It took several moments, but Rom's breathing finally

slowed, his heart calming. Beneath it, the rage was still there. It would always be there. But now he was thinking. Planning. That's what she needed from him.

"It's obvious there's something going on here," Norem said. "What I want to know is the extent to which I was successful. Hayley was supposed to be able to communicate and bond with Mindy, as you're calling her."

"We need to tell him," Rom thought.

If Hayley—the original Hayley—hadn't had so much practice schooling her expression while talking to Mindy, sharing that experience with Hayley through their shared memories, she would have gasped. Instead, she kept her face impassive as she thought, *"I won't do that to Mindy."*

"We are all getting out of here," Rom thought. *"One way or another. Mindy will be with us, so Norem won't be able to hurt her. He won't be able to hurt anyone anymore. But to stop him, I need to know what he's planning. Will you trust me?"*

She pinched her lips together. She had trusted before and had ended up here. Worse than here. The original version of herself was still out there with a different Norem. God only knew what he was doing to her now, after everything else he'd done.

"Rom is different." Hayley thought she was remembering Mindy's words from before, but she realized that the dog was listening from the other room.

"Mindy, I have to protect you," Hayley thought.

"*I have to protect you, too.*" Mindy sent a wave of warmth along with her thoughts. "*I trust Rom. We'll all keep each other safe.*"

Her heart hurt, it pounded so quickly and forcefully. She was almost dizzy from it. Bracing her feet in a strong stance, she forced herself to calm.

"I'm not telling you anything," Hayley said. Rom's eyes widened and he stepped closer to her, but she gestured for him to stay put. Instead of going to him, she took a few steps closer to Norem. The Tau Ceti who had caused her so much pain and suffering just arched an eyebrow, staring at her with curiosity.

"Unless you tell me something first," she added.

Norem's broad mouth pulled into a smirk. "And what do you want to know?"

"Where is the original Hayley?" she asked. "What have you done with her?"

"Oh…" Norem angled his head and made a tutting sound. His voice chilled as he said, "Don't overreach."

"Fine." She hadn't thought he would give her an answer to that, so now maybe he would tell her what they actually needed to know. "Then tell me why you want Mindy and me to be able to communicate telepathically. She's a dog. Most dogs aren't as intelligent as she is. It's not as though you can replace your cyborg soldiers with dogs. They don't even have opposable thumbs. What do you hope to accomplish here?"

Norem loved to brag. Hayley had managed to get information out of him before by appealing to his vanity, giving him opportunities to self-aggrandize himself with his speeches. If Rom needed to know what Norem was up to, Hayley would do everything in her power to get that information for him. Norem arched an eyebrow, not quite taking the bait.

"It's not like we're going anywhere," Hayley said.

His eyes narrowed. "The first interaction I had with a red-headed Earthling ended up with me in prison and out of favor with the brood mothers."

"And look where you are now," she coaxed. "Oh wait, you don't know where you are with your projects, because I haven't told you yet." She crossed her arms over her chest and waited.

Norem chuckled. "Well played. Alright, I don't see the harm in it. Especially since we're all going to grow old together. But I get to scan you while I disclose my nefarious plans."

"Fine." She wasted no time in crossing the room to one of the examination beds. If she hesitated, she might not be able to talk herself into doing it at all. Rom was right behind her, which helped. Her heart was still pounding and her mouth dry when she lay down on it. She stared up at the ceiling, trying to keep her panic at bay and fervently hoping that this would be worth it.

Chapter Fourteen

"I'll just be keeping my distance, if you don't mind." Norem smiled at them from across the room.

Rom wanted to punch that smile right off his face. The Tau Ceti was smart to stay out of reach. Norem took several steps away from the tank that housed Katie and started entering commands in a tablet lying on one of the counters that had already been mostly cleared. He turned and stared at the monitor above Hayley's medical bed. His brow furrowed at first, then he smiled broadly.

Even though Rom had done a quick scan of Hayley and she looked okay, he wasn't a medic in any way, shape or form. He wasn't a scientist either. Rom was a pilot. A damn good one—possibly the best—but those skills wouldn't help him here. They wouldn't help Hayley. He hated that he had to rely on Norem for information, to help keep her safe.

Maker, the irony…

"As I thought," Norem said, his attention fixated on Hayley. "You've completely stabilized. That is excellent news—for both of us. I can continue my research, and you can continue existing."

Except that Norem's research involved torturing Hayley. Maiming her. Rom wouldn't let that happen. He wouldn't let anyone ever hurt her again. They had to play along, though. Just for a little while longer.

Even if Norem got them on his ship, Rom was confident they could take it over and use it to escape. He would rather have the prism show up and help, though. For there to be any chance of that, Rom needed to stall.

"You're not holding up your end of the deal," Rom prodded. "Talk."

"Right." Norem tapped a few more commands on the tablet. "I'll use small words to help you follow along, since you don't have the benefit of my intelligence enhancers." He chuckled at his own joke, then went on.

"The life forms that developed on Earth are fascinating," Norem said. "The malleability of the DNA of every living thing on the planet is unprecedented. I discovered that human DNA can be used as a binder to introduce other species' DNA into a fully matured host." He sighed and shook his head. "I should be receiving accolades for my work." He shrugged. "No doubt, that will come in time."

"It is also incredibly easy to manipulate the DNA of Earth life forms," he continued, "such as Mindy's. Dogs have such regrettably short life spans. Fortunately, because of this, I was able to introduce my genetic agents in their parents and wait for the resulting puppies to grow to sexual maturity so I could repeat the process, creating advanced specimens in a remarkably short amount of time. Starting from an embryonic state allowed me to make much more aggressive changes as well."

Rom's hands balled into fists. His claws extended, wanting to rip into Norem's flesh. He had never hated anyone the way he hated this man.

"As you've both demonstrated quite clearly, dogs have a particular talent for working their way into the hearts of sentients," Norem said. "Even those from other planets. By facilitating strong bonds between them and the soldiers I've engineered with Cygnian DNA, I can send the animals in as scouts. Dogs naturally ingratiate themselves with others. Once they're deeply entrenched, we will use the transit platforms to send wave after wave of soldiers through blue space right into the heart of any facility, civilization, or outpost we desire. We'll be unstoppable, and they'll never see us coming."

"Tarn was right, but it's even worse than we thought." Rom didn't intend to send the message to Hayley, but she picked it up anyway.

"Tarn?"

"A member of my prism. Our engineer. He figured out that the Tau Centauran Assembly was herding survivors from the Sadirian settlements they've been attacking into the Sol system. He thought they planned to use the transit platform on Ceres to bring in soldiers. But if Norem's plan

works, they won't even need that. And after they conquer the Sol system, they'll be able to take over any other system they want."

"I would love to play poker with you, Cygnian," Norem said. "Your face is an open book. I can see that you're beginning to understand the genius of my plan. Mindy's siblings have scattered all over Earth. Once I figure out the details of the bonding my soldiers will need, I can implant the programming within them and teleport contingent after contingent to the planet. Not even the Vegans will be able to stand against our numbers."

Rom's stomach felt leaden. His hearts raced and his spine plates vibrated furiously. Norem was correct, unfortunately. If they could make this plan work, Earth was doomed. And after that, Rom had no doubt that the Tau Ceti would spread like a plague throughout the universe, devouring worlds—and their inhabitants—with impunity.

"We'll stop you," Rom said.

"How?" The panel next to Norem beeped. He glanced down and smiled. "Our ride is here. You've done a lovely job stalling, but we really do need to be on our way."

A trio of scientists headed toward the tank holding Katie. Norem lashed out, quick as a snake, and grabbed one by his arm. He jerked the man back, almost making him fall.

"Did you check your pockets?" Norem asked. "The

others did."

The man's face paled to a putrid green. Norem's eyes rolled up to the ceiling.

"I'm surrounded by idiots." He released his grip, but only to reach into the man's pocket with one hand. The whole time, he kept his grip on that damned triggering device.

If only he would put it down, even for a moment. Rom would be on him so quickly, Norem wouldn't know what hit him. Norem pulled a small scanning device out of the other Tau Ceti's pocket, then held it up and wiggled it in front of his face.

"I am so close to the next stage of my work," Norem said. "I will not have anyone messing this up for me. Is that clear?"

The man nodded nervously, then backed away a few steps. Giving Norem a wide berth, he hurried to the tank to help the others disconnect it from its moorings. Norem huffed out a puff of breath, his lips curled in a sneer of disgust. He strolled to a nearby table and picked up a device Rom didn't recognize.

"Surrounded," Norem paused for effect, looking at Rom and Hayley, "by idiots."

He pointed the device at the man who had almost approached the tank with a scanner. A bolt of yellow energy fired out from it. The man shrieked as it hit him, his skin vaporizing as the energy burned a hole through his body.

"Stop," Rom yelled, but it was too late. Hayley screamed and rolled off the examination table, clinging to Rom's side.

Norem deactivated the device just before the man's lifeless body fell to the floor. He didn't even look at the man he'd killed. Merely examined the instrument he'd used to kill him.

"Not its intended function, but it gets the job done." Norem set the laser down on the counter next to him. "I always find a way to get the job done. You'll learn that about me during our travels."

The two remaining scientists finished disconnecting Katie's tank. Panic built in Rom's chest. It took him a moment to realize it was Hayley's.

"*We need to escape,*" she thought. "*Now. Once we're on the ship, it will be so much harder for the prism to find us.*"

"*It's going to be okay.*" Rom sent calming emotions along with the words. "*The prism can find me, even if we're on the move. They'll just split up so they can triangulate our position better. With six ships, I know they'll find us eventually. It'll take time, and I don't want Norem to be able to keep up with his 'work' while they're looking for us.*"

He felt Hayley's shudder as much as he saw it. Norem noticed, too.

"Your turn," Norem said. "Talk as you walk. You two first—and be sure to pick up Mindy along the way—then K-0. Be sure to speak up since I'll be way in the back, keeping an eye on everyone."

Dammit. Norem was going to make this hard for them.

"*Getting to the ship is a good thing*," Rom thought, being sure to project to Mindy as well. "*I'm the best pilot in the Cygnian fleet. We find our moment, tear through their crew, and we can fly ourselves back to Earth.*"

"*I like that idea,*" Mindy thought.

"*Then be ready to go,*" Rom thought. "*Hayley?*"

She looked at Rom and nodded, reaching out to grip his hand tight. They headed to the door together, but didn't speak until they were in the hallway. Three more soldiers waited for them. The men turned and led the way down the hall, also keeping their distance and eyeing Rom warily.

Hayley paused in front of the door to the bathroom. It slid open and Mindy slowly walked out. Her head was low and her tail wagged slowly behind her, though it was tucked between her legs. Hayley buried her fingers in Mindy's ruff.

"You don't hurt her," Hayley said, looking at Norem over her shoulder. True to his word, the Tau Ceti was hanging way back, Katie's tank blocking much of the hallway between them as it floated along with the help of an antigravity device. "Whatever information you need, whatever data or tests, you are not allowed to hurt her. Do you understand?"

"Mindy has never once felt pain because of me," Norem said. "To do so would negate her value to my experiment. I need her happy and able to bond with my soldiers, not remembering trauma associated with them."

"*Is that true?*" Hayley thought.

"*It is.*" Mindy's thought. "*No one has ever hurt me.*"

Hayley let out a shaky breath. She turned, keeping one hand in Mindy's fur and gripping Rom's hand tight with her other. They headed down the hall as Hayley began to speak.

"She's much smarter than other dogs," Hayley said. "I expect you already know that."

"Of course," Norem said. "It was the first thing I tested for and the easiest change to make. You'll be happy to know that an interesting side-effect of increasing her intelligence and that of her relatives seems to be an extended lifespan."

An unexpected wave of happiness flowed through Hayley. Rom felt it, too. He held onto it, amplifying her emotion. They could use the boost, with everything going on around them. Plus, it gave them even more to fight for. Mindy's tail rose a bit and she held her head higher.

"Thank you, Norem," Norem said, in a high, mocking voice. "I'm so glad I get to be with my beloved dog for many more years than I expected."

Hayley's lips curled up and Mindy growled.

"We'd be more grateful if we knew you'd done it on purpose," Hayley sneered. "Except the shorter lifespan of big dogs was part of their draw for you. You admitted it yourself."

"I suppose." Norem chuckled. "Now, is that 'we' you and Rom or you and Mindy? I've never been quite sure just how intelligent she is or whether she can understand me or not."

Hayley didn't want to go on. Rom could feel it. But she also didn't want to break her word, even to the man who had tormented her and was still torturing her friend. Rom admired her honor and absolutely understood her reluctance to continue. But if Rom had his way, this Norem would die before he had a chance to update anyone on what Mindy could do. Rom was already formulating a plan, figuring out the best time to make his move. And even if the other Norems found out what Mindy could do, she would be with Rom and the other Cygnians. They could keep her safe.

"*Tell him,*" Rom thought.

"*I'm keeping Mindy out of it as much as I can,*" Hayley responded. "*I only agreed to explain what I can do.*"

"*Fair enough,*" Rom thought.

"Dog thoughts are different than human thoughts," Hayley mused. It wasn't a lie, in the most general sense of the words. "When I—" She winced. "When the original Hayley arrived at Ceres, she told you that she sensed a presence in her mind, but that she didn't know who or what it was. It was just a feeling."

"I already know that," Norem said. "That's why I risked taking her in the first place. Give me something new, H-7. I'm growing impatient."

"It was more than a feeling," Hayley said. "Much more. She and Mindy began communicating then."

Norem cut in. "Yes, through shared emotions, which I amplified through my experiments while augmenting her DNA. I need to know how successful the changes were."

"They had nothing to do with how we communicate," Hayley said, looking down at Mindy. "We could already speak to each other in our minds."

"Wait... in words?" Norem's tone was incredulous.

Hayley looked up at Rom, her eyes pinched with worry. He nodded his reassurance and squeezed her hand.

"*It's okay,*" Mindy thought to them. "*You can tell him. He won't hurt me. He's right that I have to trust to form bonds.*"

Hayley nodded. "With words."

"My, my," Norem said. "She's even more magnificent than I thought."

Mindy let out a dismissive chuff.

"The bond she forms is based on trust," Hayley said. "If you or your soldiers ever harm her, she'll never trust you and you'll never be able to bond with her and use her to travel, no matter what you do to her DNA."

This time, Norem was the one to let out a brief laugh. "You think I don't already know that? Why do you think I've executed anyone who has so much as said an unkind word to her? Why do you think I never retaliated, even when she bit off my fingers multiple times."

Rom smiled down at Mindy and muttered, "Good girl." The dog's mouth opened in a toothy grin.

"Enough with the mutual admiration," Norem said. "We've arrived. I want to know more about this, so we will have to continue our discussions once everyone is settled."

Rom's hearts pounded as they walked through the large double-doors in front of them. He could tell they were on a ship the moment he set foot on it. There was a lightness, an agility to a ship that stations just didn't have. He glanced all around, trying to figure out what he could work with.

The design wasn't Tau Ceti. That was a good thing. A very good thing. Tau Ceti ships were clunky—except for their small fighters. They won because of their numbers and disregard for the lives of their soldiers, not their superior skill nor advanced tech. The walls of the ship they were on were pale gray with a red line bisecting it and running parallel to the darker gray deck. This was a Centauran vessel.

His prism had made contact with a Centauran who might be able to help broker peace between his people and the Coalition, which could stop the war raging through the galaxy. Rom didn't want to do anything to screw that up. At the same time, he would do whatever it took to keep Hayley, Mindy, and Katie safe.

He could do this. *They* could do this. Working together, he knew they would find a way to escape. He prayed to the Maker that he was right.

Chapter Fifteen

"We need to check in with the captain," Norem said. "The Centaurans insist on having one of theirs at the head of all their ships now, but the rest of this crew are all Tau Ceti. They're all mine. And, in case you get any ideas, there's what the Earthling's call a 'dead-man's switch' on this device. Such a clever phrase—and an even more clever concept. If I die, a fatal charge builds in K-0's tank. Shouldn't take more than a few seconds. Your Cygnian friend might think to smash the tank to get her out in time, but with how cramped the space is, I doubt you could succeed without grievously injuring her or even killing her yourself."

Norem chuckled. "Let's all just avoid that moral conundrum and play nice. As soon as we're done with the captain, we can all get comfy in our labs. K-0 will have to accompany us for the time being, of course. Until you both realize that I will inflict pain—and damage—on her whenever necessary to keep you in line."

"*What are we going to do?*" Hayley's grip on Rom's hand tightened.

"*Bide our time,*" he thought back. "*Wait for our*

opportunity and do everything we can to help my prism find us. They're working on getting the Centaurans to sever ties with the Tau Ceti as well. That might work to our advantage, if they succeed."

"*The entire crew is Tau Ceti, except for the captain,*" Hayley thought.

Mindy let out a whine and butted Hayley's free hand with her nose. Hayley rested her head on the dog's scruff instinctively.

"*It'll be okay,*" she thought to them both. "*Won't it?*"

Knowing that at least Mindy was safe from Norem—as safe as anyone could be—Hayley didn't feel like she was lying when she replied, "*It will. We'll get through this.*"

She forced herself to believe the thought-speak and found that she walked with her back a bit straighter, her head higher. Rom might have noticed the difference in her, because he also squared his shoulders, glancing down at her with a smile as he sent warmth through their bond. Somehow, she returned it and meant it. They were going to get through this, together.

They passed through the docking bay, walking silently down corridor after corridor, deeper into the ship. Finally, another broad set of doors opened before them, revealing what she thought must be the bridge. Four men were inside. Three sat at sleek command kiosks, the workstations' tops curving in graceful arcs. The bulky builds of the men, along with their identical haircuts, gave them away as Tau Ceti soldiers as clearly as their uniforms. They barely glanced at Hayley and her odd party.

The fourth man was already standing off to one side, his arms crossed over his wide chest as he stared at the viewscreen. His pale blond hair was longer, pulled back in a tie, but would brush his shoulders when loose. His jaw was chiseled and clean-shaven, his eyes a piercing green. They widened slightly and his lips parted when he turned to them and saw her, but the expression vanished so quickly, she wasn't sure what she had seen. Focus and command settled over his features.

"Take stations," he snapped at the three soldiers accompanying their group. "If you're going to be on my ship, you're going to work."

They looked to Norem, who nodded. The triad of soldiers hurried to various points at the bridge's bulkhead and began tapping command buttons and attending to data scrolling on small screens at their workstations. Norem kept his smile in place, but Hayley could see how the skin around his eyes tightened. He pressed a button on his bracer and Katie's tank slowly settled to the floor.

"You have ten seconds to explain why you have someone in a tank before I escort you to an airlock and let you find another transport," the captain said.

"*I kinda like this guy,*" Rom thought. Mindy chuffed a broad-mouthed laugh.

Something about him had Hayley's skin crawling. An awareness that wasn't quite right. It was probably that he was flippantly talking about killing Norem, and if that happened, Katie would follow. Norem still held the device in his hand and was keeping his distance. That only put him closer to the captain, who seemed to like him about as much as they did.

"She's insurance," Norem said. "The only thing keeping this Cygnian prisoner from destroying your ship and killing everyone on it is the woman in this tank." Norem held up the device. "He doesn't behave, she suffers for it."

The captain's lips curled up in a sneer. He shook his head and turned away.

"*The Centaurans entered the war because of experiments the High Council conducted on their people,*" Rom thought. "*They can't stand anyone experimenting on other life forms.*"

"*Can we use that to our advantage here?*" Hayley wondered.

"*If we tell him the truth, it'll only get the captain killed,*" Rom thought back. "*He's surrounded by enemies and he doesn't even know it.*"

"I don't like how you Tau Ceti operate," the captain commented.

Maybe he had a better idea of it than they thought.

Norem closed the distance between them, standing at

the captain's side. "We still get the job done."

"Captain, we've reached a safe distance," one of the men seated at the command kiosks said.

The captain nodded curtly. "On screen."

A station filled the viewscreen. Three dark bronze rings surrounded a central blob that resembled a half-melted mushroom. Hayley shuddered as she recognized the Tau Ceti design. That was where she'd been held. Where she'd been tormented... and probably created.

"Proceed," the captain said. "Maximum power to shields."

Moments later, the screen filled with light. The deck beneath them shifted as a wave of force blew out from somewhere—from where the station used to be. Hayley blinked against the fading light. Bits of debris floated past their view against the dark backdrop of space.

Norem turned to them and smiled. "It's standard procedure when a base is compromised. When your prism arrives, they'll find no clues about where we're heading. No glimpses into our plans."

"They will find you," Rom growled. "And when they do, they will make you pay for all you've done."

Norem laughed, a broad smile stretching his face. "Your prism doesn't scare me. I've had Hayley for months while the most notorious Scorpiian in the universe searched for her. If he can't find me, no one can. I am untouchable."

His smile vanished as his mouth dropped open, his eyes widening in shock. He looked over his shoulder at the captain, who had lashed out more rapidly than Hayley could track, and now stood right behind Norem, the fingers of one hand on Norem's shoulder, digging into his flesh.

"Might want to rethink that," the captain said, in a low even voice.

Behind them, electricity blasted out from the command stations, wrapping around the Tau Ceti soldiers stationed there. The men jerked and spasmed uncontrollably, smoke rising from their bodies and filling the room with a horrible stench. Hayley covered her mouth as she retched, the men falling lifelessly to the deck. The air processors kicked in, circulating the air and filtering away the scent of charred flesh.

Mindy started barking at Norem and the captain, the fur along her spine standing up like Rom's spine plates. Wave after wave of nauseating goosebumps coated Hayley's body. This couldn't be happening. This couldn't be—

Norem made a gurgling sound as his face became puffy, snakelike rivulets squirming beneath his skin. Silver liquid dribbled from the corners of his eyes and mouth. The captain's face twisted in a rage unlike anything Hayley had ever seen before, contorting until he was unrecognizable—until he... was.

"You dared to take what's mine," the captain said, his

skin glowing silver. "Now I'm taking what's yours. Your ship. Your work. Your life."

Norem let out one last gasp and went limp before he fell to the deck, a gaping hole in his back. The silver liquid retreated, flowing over his body toward the man standing behind him. It pooled at the man's feet, flowing up his legs and merging with his clothing. The silver light emanating from him faded. He ran a shaking hand through what was now his disheveled, short brown hair. His other arm hung at his side—still silver. Norem's blood dripped from its sharp, gleaming point. It morphed back to a regular hand as he looked up at her, his soulful brown eyes filled with pain and regret.

"Dean..." Hayley whispered.

Chapter Sixteen

Fuck. This was not happening. Rom was not about to face off with the most terrifying adversary they'd ever faced—with no backup. Rom's spine plates were up and vibrating as though they were trying to lift his feet from the ground. Hayley was frozen with fear, and as far as Rom knew, she wasn't even aware of all the new things Dean—better known as Zakarri now—could do. Hell, he'd taken out every single augmented Tau Ceti soldier on the bridge at once. Rom was certain they'd find nothing but Tau Ceti bodies throughout the rest of the ship. He'd killed them all without touching them.

Except for Norem. No, Zakarri had chosen to kill Norem up close and personal. Slowly. Horribly. Painfully.

Mindy started barking. Not at Dean, but at Rom. She let out a piercing, plaintive whine. Wait, dogs couldn't make a noise like that.

"Oh shit," he said. "Katie's tank."

Rom ran to it, trying to find a way in without hurting her. Norem had been correct. If Rom tried to force it, he could easily kill her himself. Katie was awake, her eyes wild with fear, though her pupils were still dilated from the neuro-suppressants she'd been given. She couldn't keep the tech from killing her. Rom gripped the top of the tank, trying to pry it off.

"There's a dead-man's switch keyed to Norem," Rom yelled. "It's on the deck."

He wasn't sure why he was bothering. It wasn't like Dean would help. Silver light glinted off the tank's glass. Rom looked over his shoulder to see Norem—no, Dean—stoop down and pick the device up off the floor. He pressed the button, sending a shock through Katie. This close, Rom could hear her scream, even muffled through the liquid.

"What the hell are you doing?" Rom yelled.

"Resetting it," Dean-Norem snapped, hurrying closer. As he did, spindly silver legs erupted from his torso, lifting him high off the floor. Another set of arms pushed out from his chest, each ending in deadly-sharp pincers. "Hold the tank steady."

Rom wasn't sure he could hold *himself* steady while staring down this monster. He ducked down low, on eye-level with Katie, and wrapped his arms around the tank. She wasn't being shocked anymore, but the terror on her face as she stared at the nightmare-Norem approaching her would haunt Rom forever.

"It's okay," Rom yelled. "He's going to help."

Rom couldn't believe what he was saying. Either way, he hoped it eased Katie's fear. Without Dean's help, Rom couldn't deceive himself that they would be able to save her. He had to put his faith in his enemy.

Dean-Norem reached the tank, the device carefully held in one of his relatively normal-looking hands. With his two silver arms, he gripped the top of the tank, then twisted and pulled. The pincers sliced through the transparent material right at the top joint as if it was nothing. Rom had used all his strength while attempting to separate them, and it hadn't budged.

Once the lid was off, Dean tossed it aside, then rose up higher on those thin, spider-like legs. He reached down into the tank, his pincers morphing into another set of skin-covered, humanoid hands. Katie screamed again, bubbles erupting around her mask. She pushed herself deeper into the tank, trying to get away from Dean.

"It's okay," Rom shouted. "He won't... he won't hurt you."

Katie glanced at Rom, eyes still wild with fear. She was too smart not to have noticed his hesitation. She looked past Rom to Hayley. Rom looked at Hayley questioningly. Hayley nodded.

Katie slowly nodded back, then straightened, bringing herself closer to Dean's outstretched arms. She shuddered when he touched her, but didn't fight as he lifted her from the tank. Viscous liquid flowed down the sides of the glass, but Rom maintained his grip on the tank until she was free. He stared up at Dean, hearts pounding, wondering what surprise would pop out next.

"He won't hurt you," Hayley said in a thready voice. "Because you're my friend and he knows it would hurt me if anything happened to you."

Dean-Norem frowned. He pulled Katie closer, then took a few steps away, easing them both to the ground. The spindly legs pulled back into his body. He crushed the device and tossed it away, then reabsorbed his 'regular' arms as well. The arms he was using to hold Katie shifted position, his entire body glowing. By the time he set her on the floor—with surprising gentleness—he was back to looking like himself. Rather, his most common assumed form. He was back to being Dean.

"I won't hurt her because I know what it's like to be trapped in a tank and experimented on by people who don't care about your pain and see you as nothing more than a data set to manipulate," Dean said. He carefully removed the mask from Katie's face, helping her to lean forward as she coughed and sputtered. Looking at Rom, he said, "Get two of their jackets."

Right. Katie would want to be covered. Rom quickly complied, only wondering about the second jacket as he handed Dean the first. The Scorpiian assassin responsible for countless deaths, who had destroyed the ecosystems of entire planets, took it and gently wiped away the worst of the liquid still clinging to Katie's skin. He stood, bringing her with him as if she weighed nothing, and set her on her feet. Rom draped the still-dry jacket over her shoulders, holding on to help her stand.

"Th…thank you," she said, leaning against Rom.

Dean didn't say anything. He turned to face Hayley. Rom was about to step forward, to do… something. He wasn't sure what. But Hayley's voice was already in his mind.

"*Don't,*" she thought. "*Let me handle this.*"

"*Be careful,*" Rom replied. "*We don't know how he'll react when he finds out…*"

"*That I'm not who he thinks I am.*"

The sadness that went along with the thought wasn't as intense as Rom expected. He hoped that meant she was accepting it—accepting herself. And he really, really hoped that Dean would accept who and what she was as well. If they played this wrong and Dean found out they were bonded soulmates before he understood that she wasn't *his* Hayley… Rom looked around at the bodies surrounding them and suppressed a shudder.

Dean wasn't having as much luck with that. He was visibly trembling as he took a step closer to Hayley. His hand shook violently as he ran it through his hair again.

"I…" he began. "I'm so sorry. I didn't mean for any of this to happen. Everything I've done, I did to try to find you. Please, you have to believe—"

"Dean." Hayley spoke his name sharply. She hesitated, before she slowly approached him. What was she doing?

She should be keeping her distance in case he freaked out when he learned the truth. Instead, she stopped right in front of him.

"Look at me," she said. "Really look at me."

Dean intently scrutinized her face, studying her features. At first, all Rom saw was longing, until Dean's brow furrowed and confusion swept over him. Rom readied himself, not that he could do much against the Scorpiian. The best he could hope for would be to stall him while the others ran away.

"Do you remember the garnet and silver earrings?" Hayley said. "Your one-month anniversary gift?"

Dean reached up and gently tucked her hair behind her ear. His hand wasn't shaking anymore. As he started to lift his hand away, she grasped it, pressing it against her cheek.

"My ears aren't pierced," she whispered with a catch in her voice, her eyes filling with tears. "My freckles are gone. And my scars. The ones on my body, anyway. I remember everything. And I understand now. How your pant legs weren't wet from the rain until I mentioned it that first night. How you offered to show me the galaxy— the universe. How you offered your heart, before I was ready. Before *she* was ready."

Dean closed his eyes and lowered his head, shaking it. "No. No."

"I'm not her," Hayley said. "I'm not Hayley. I'm not

your Hayley. The woman you hope will be yours."

"No," Dean repeated. "Please, no."

When Dean looked at her again, Rom's hearts clenched, his breath rushing from him as if he'd been struck. He had thought he'd experienced despair before, wondering if he would ever find his soulmate. Now, this intense agony on Dean's face told a different story. Rom had never known that level of hopelessness. He'd never known a universe without a glimmer of light.

"What did he do to her to make you?" Dean murmured, scanning Hayley's face as if searching for answers. "Are you all that's left?"

Rom's spine plates vibrated even more intensely. Would Dean want Hayley to stay with him? Would he try to claim her as his own? And if so, how could Rom stop him?

"She's still out there," Hayley reassured him. "She's still alive. We can sense her."

Dean's features twisted with fresh pain. "With Norem? While he's doing things like *this* to her?" Dean looked Hayley up and down, then shook his head. "It's almost better if she were—"

"Don't even say it," Hayley cut in. "She's holding on. She's doing what she has to do in order to survive. You need to do the same."

"I'll never find her now." Dean pulled away from Hayley and stepped back. His hands were shaking again and ripples of silver light swept over his skin.

"*Hayley…*" Rom warned.

"This was my last lead," Dean said. "My last hope. Even if I find her, the amount of biomass Norem would need to make a clone that could hold her memories… What he must have done to her to make it happen…"

The pulses of light quickened, intensified. Dean dropped to his knees, wrapping his arms around his middle. He rocked back and forth, shaking his head. His skin rippled, nubs of appendages appearing and disappearing from his torso, his features morphing from the captain's to Norem's and through dozens of other faces that Rom didn't recognize.

"She'll never forgive me," he said, his voice distorted as his throat changed form yet again. Dean was curled in a ball, it was as if he was collapsing in on himself. With the way his body was changing uncontrollably, maybe he would. Spikes and spines shot out from him, quicksilver oozing from wherever they emerged. He cried out in pain as his body began to tear itself apart.

"*This is our chance,*" Rom thought. "*We have to get away while we can.*"

"*No.*" Hayley shook her head. "*I can't leave him like this.*"

"*Hayley,*" Rom near-shouted in his mind.

"*She cared for him,*" Hayley thought back. "*The original Hayley. She might have loved him, if things had gone differently. I have to do this. For her.*"

Rom wanted to argue, but he knew there was no point. As much as he was terrified for her, he had to respect her choice.

"*Be careful,*" he thought. "*I love you.*"

"*I love you, too.*"

Hayley dropped to her knees next to Dean and wrapped her arms around him, as if she could hold him together. Maybe she could, because the spikes stopped appearing. He still bucked and writhed, but she only held on tighter.

"Dean," she said. "You have to stop. She needs you. *I* need you. We have to work together if we're going to save her."

"She's gone," Dean shouted, his voice distorted almost beyond understanding.

"She's not. I can feel her. I know she's out there. She's changed, but she's stronger. Norem has no idea what he's done in making her what she is."

"What is she?" The erratic shifts of Dean's body slowed a bit.

"A survivor," Hayley said. "She's holding on. You have to as well."

Long moments dragged on as Hayley held on to him, his movements slowing to a few twitches. The silver light bathing his body faded, leaving the lanky human form Rom was most used to seeing. Dean looked up at Hayley, beads of quicksilver coating his face. He was panting, even though he didn't truly need breath.

"Things didn't work out the way any of us hoped," Hayley whispered. "That doesn't mean they're hopeless now. You found me on your own. *I* can feel her. We can work together to find her."

"*Tell him about me.*" Mindy stepped forward and barked once, her tail wagging slowly behind her.

"*Mindy, I don't know if that's a good idea*," Hayley thought.

"*Please*," Mindy thought.

Hayley looked to Rom. He said, "It's her choice."

"What's whose choice?" Katie blinked rapidly and shook her head as if to clear it. She listed to the side, but Rom kept her upright. At least she was talking. Hopefully, that meant whatever Norem had put in her system was wearing off.

Hayley turned back to Dean. "Did Norem ever tell you about his MIN-D project?"

"No," Dean said. "I knew about it anyway."

Hayley couldn't suppress her grin. That was a glimpse of the Dean she remembered—original Hayley remembered. Her smile faltered.

"Well, Norem didn't know that he succeeded," Hayley said. "Mindy and Hayley connected. That's why he took Hayley in the first place."

A muscle in Dean's jaw began to twitch. Damn, it was uncanny how well he could replicate human emotion. Rom would never guess he was a Scorpiian if he hadn't already known.

"*Tell him this,*" Mindy thought. "*Tell him that if he doesn't believe you can help find Hayley, he knows that I can. Hayley is my friend, too, and I'm not going to stop looking for her.*"

Hayley laughed and reached out, petting Mindy's shoulder and bringing her closer for a hug. She kept her other arm around Dean. Rom wasn't surprised when the Scorpiian reached out and pulled Mindy into a group embrace. They knew he had a soft spot for animals after he'd spared an entire space station at the request of one of the space-kittens he'd befriended.

"I heard her," Dean said, his eyes wide with wonder. "I heard her in my mind."

"*Shit, can he hear us, too?*" Rom thought.

"*No, only me.*" Mindy looked up at Rom over her shoulder. "*I think I'm getting stronger, too. I'm learning to control what I can do. I wanted him to hear me, really bad, so he did.*"

"*We should still be careful,*" Rom thought to Hayley.

Mindy turned back to Dean and stared at him intently. "*I will go with you,*" she thought clearly. "*To help you find my first-friend-Hayley.*"

Dean's eyes widened. Rom was sure he'd heard that, too.

"What?" Hayley said out loud. "No. No! You can't."

Mindy whined and leaned over to lick Hayley's cheek. *"New-friend-Hayley can feel her, too. Rom said his prism can find him better if they split up and feel where he is from different directions. If we both look for her from different places, it'll help us find her."*

Damn, she was right. But Rom didn't like the idea of her going off with the Scorpiian. He didn't trust Dean.

"I know you're worried," Mindy thought. *"But Dean understands. He was alone, just as I was, until first-friend-Hayley. She made us both feel... togetherness. Not alone. He understands. He'll take care of me."* She leaned over and licked Dean's cheek gently. *"We'll take care of each other."*

Dean released Hayley and wrapped his arms around Mindy, pulling her close. He buried his face against her neck, her fur muffling the sound of him crying. Rom's hearts clenched. He reached down and clasped Dean's shoulder, despite himself. Despite everything the assassin had done. In that moment, he had never known his enemy to be so... human. Hayley rested her hand on Dean's other shoulder.

After a moment, Katie threw her arm out, her hand awkwardly patting Dean's head.

"I'm not sure what's going on," Katie said almost drunkenly. "But, I'm here for it."

Rom chuckled, he couldn't help it. Hayley joined in and he could hear Mindy's laugh in his mind. When Dean looked up, even his lips were quirked up on one side. He wiped at his face with his arm, pulling himself together with an obvious effort.

"I swear on my life, I will keep you safe," Dean said, scratching behind Mindy's ears. "And even though..." His voice cracked, but he kept going. "I know Hayley can never forgive me for my part in what's happened to her, I won't give up until I find her. I'll bring her home."

Chapter Seventeen

"The prism is here." Rom thought the words directly to Hayley. She wasn't sure why.

"We should let Dean know so he doesn't attack them," Hayley thought.

"I will, but you should know that Sophie is with them."

It took a moment for Hayley to process what he was communicating. Then her stomach bottomed out with panic. As hard as it had been to talk to Dean about being a clone, it would be a thousand times worse with Sophie. A million.

"What?" Fear laced Hayley's unspoken reply. *"How did she know I was with you?"*

"That's not why she's here. She's Lar's soulmate. He's another Cygnian in my prism. Amy and Becca have bonded with two of the others."

Hayley looked at Rom and just sort of blinked as her brain tried to make sense of what he was saying. The most unbelievable part wasn't that they had all bonded with Cygnian soulmates. It was that Becca had bonded with anyone at all. Her notoriously high standards had been a constant source of teasing among her sisters. Becca had never found anyone worthy of bringing into their family, who she placed above everyone.

"*Becca?*" Hayley repeated.

"*She bonded with the crown prince.*"

"*The crown prince of your entire people?*" Hayley asked.

"*Yes.*"

"*Okay... I guess that tracks.*" Finally, someone who met her standards. "*Is Sophie going to be running through that big open door any second?*"

"*I don't know,*" Rom thought. "*She might be staying on the ship to protect those who are expecting.*"

"*Expecting what?*"

A wave of warmth flowed to her through their bond. Warmth and longing and affection and so much more. It only took a moment of that for her to realize what he meant.

"*Oh...*" Excitement edged out Hayley's fear. "*Is Sophie...?*"

"*Not yet, but she and Lar are working on it.*"

Hayley snorted. "*I don't doubt it. What about Becca and Amy?*"

"*Becca and Kral aren't pregnant yet, but Amy and Dorn are.*"

"Amy?" she squealed, the sound making her realize she'd spoken out loud. She couldn't help herself, though. Amy was like a sister to her—a baby sister. The idea of her having a child of her own was more than she could contain. The joy bubbling up in Hayley suddenly clouded as she remembered that Amy wasn't like a little sister to her. That relationship was with the original Hayley.

"What the fuck was that about?" Katie said blearily. "High-pitched noises hurt my head."

"We'll get you checked out here in a minute." Rom looked to Dean and said, "Head's up—a group of Cygnian warriors are about to charge through that door. I'd take it as a show of good faith if you didn't attack them."

"I won't." Dean stood, but kept one hand on Mindy's ruff.

"They might not extend you the same favor," Hayley said.

"I know." Dean backed farther from the door. Mindy went with him.

As Rom had said, a moment later, a trio of blue giants pounded through the door. They paused with their feet braced, arms up and ready to attack. When no one made a move, they lowered their arms, glancing around in confusion. One had pale white hair that flowed around his shoulders. His skin was a lighter shade of blue as well and his eyes gleamed a beautiful emerald-green. Another was a deep cobalt blue, his dark blue hair hanging down his back in intricate braids and his eyes bright yellow.

The Cygnian in front… Hayley was certain without a doubt that he was Kral. His skin was sapphire blue, his hair a shade darker. He had a beard that matched his wild mane of hair and his eyes glowed orange like twin burning suns. They were all giants—at least seven feet tall, like Rom, but this one was thick with muscle. She'd never seen such an enormous man in her life. He exuded command as he surveyed the room, his eyes skimming over her and locking on Dean.

"Rom," Kral said. "How concerned should I be that the most dangerous mercenary in the known galaxy is standing behind you… petting a dog?"

"Only mildly," Rom said.

The white-haired Cygnian snorted. "I'm more concerned for the criminal. When Queenie finds out he has another animal companion, she's going to kill him herself."

"*Queenie?*" Hayley thought to Rom.

"*She's a super-intelligent Earth kitten born on a spacecraft,*" Rom replied. "*It's… a long story. Just know that she's remarkably intimidating.*"

"*A kitten?*"

"*You'll see when you meet her. She lives with Dorn and Amy. That's Dorn with the green eyes. The one with the yellow is Lar. Kral is—*"

"*The one with orange eyes. I figured that much out.*"

Rom sent a wave of approval through their bond. It was all the time they had to communicate before the others spoke again.

"Queenie knows no one could ever take her place in my heart," Dean said, calmly.

"Funny," Lar began, "I didn't know you had one."

Dean smirked and added, "Only when necessary."

"Enough banter," Kral said. "Rom, are you well?"

"I am." Rom tried to step forward, but Katie was still swaying in his arms.

"Let me," Dean said. The moment he moved, the other Cygnians dropped right back into their crouches, arms raised and fierce expressions on their faces.

"It's okay," Rom said. He lifted Katie and carried her to Dean. The Scorpiian let him tuck her against his side, holding her up against him. She nestled in and her eyes drifted shut.

Kral, Lar, and Dorn straightened, casting wary glances to each other. Now that Rom was unburdened, he was able to approach. As soon as he was in arm's reach, the other men grasped him and pulled him into an embrace. Hayley could feel their tension fading. She could feel… them. All of them. Mostly, she felt Rom's relief, but there were clear echoes of the emotion coming from each of the other Cygnians. It was so strange.

"The soulmate bond allows us to feel each other's emotions," Rom said, turning back to her with one arm still over Kral's shoulder. The prince had his arm wrapped around Rom's waist. "And the prism bond lets us feel each other as well, to a lesser degree. As my soulmate, you are connected to them also."

"You found your soulmate?" Lar said. He turned to Hayley, beaming.

"I did." The pride flowing from Rom brought tears to Hayley's eyes. No matter what else happened, she would hold on to that feeling. His acceptance and belonging and love. She was glad to have that anchor for what came next.

"This is Hayley," he said.

All three Cygnian's gasped, their eyes widening. She would have felt their joy even without any sort of bond. It only took her a moment to realize that it was misplaced. Rom's smile faded as he sensed her panic.

"You found Hayley," Lar said, his voice filled with wonder.

"Wait, it's not—" Before Rom could finish his statement, the command kiosks on the bridge exploded.

Mindy yelped, ducking behind Dean. The Scorpiian wheeled around, tucking Katie in close and pulling Mindy closer as he transformed into a huge beast with a thick hide. Sparks showered around him, skittering harmlessly to the ground. Rom leapt across the room in one giant stride, landing next to Hayley and pulling her close. He wrapped himself around her, shielding him from the electricity raining around them.

"What is with blowing up?" Hayley shouted.

"Scorpiian," Rom yelled as Dean glowed silver and

returned to his usual form.

"It isn't him." Was that Lar who had spoken?

Hayley peered out from beneath Rom's protective embrace and saw Lar stepping forward, lightning arcing from the kiosks to his outstretched arms. His spine plates were standing up straight, electricity lighting them up from within.

"Holy crap," Hayley thought. *"Can your spine plates do that?"*

"No. Lar and Sophie were altered by our Maker goddess."

"Sophie?" Dread pitted Hayley's stomach. *"Altered how? Is she okay?"*

"She's more than okay," Rom replied. *"But she's also more than she was before."*

Hayley didn't get a chance to ask for more information. She didn't need to. The lighting swirling in front of Lar coalesced into a silhouette of a woman. The light drew together, becoming more solid, so bright, Hayley squinted her eyes against it, but she couldn't bring herself to look away. In a final burst, the light faded, leaving Sophie standing in Lar's arms.

"Love, how did you do that?" Lar's eyes were wide with wonder.

Sophie pushed him away. She turned around, surveying the room with wide eyes. The kiosks crackled and sputtered, their contours no more than blackened husks.

She saw the flash of Katie's red hair and took a step forward, then paused, scanning the room again until her eyes locked with Hayley's.

"Hayley?" Her voice wavered. "Hayley, is that you?"

Hayley's heart beat hard and fast. Her throat was too tight to form words. She shook her head instead.

Sophie took another step forward. Sophie, who had snuck into Hayley's room when she was staying with the Myers family after Hayley's mom had died, crawling into bed with her to comfort her when they were both children. Sophie, who had excitedly told Hayley about her first kiss. Sophie, who had been there for Hayley for almost as long as she could remember.

Remembrance of memories that weren't hers.

"Hayley!" Sophie smiled, tears streaming down her cheeks as she rushed forward.

Rom blocked her way.

The scent of ozone flooded Hayley's senses. She heard crackling behind Sophie's back and could see the crest of a spine plate made of pure energy. Holy shit! What had happened to her?

"Cygnian, you have one second to move before I move you," Sophie said.

A chill swept down Hayley's back. She hadn't known her friend could sound so intimidating. More than her form must have changed since Hayley was taken.

"He's trying to protect you," Hayley said, finally

finding her voice.

"From what?" Sophie craned her neck, trying to get a better look at Hayley. "Are you okay? Are you hurt? What did Norem do to you?"

Hayley pinched her lips together in a straight line, trying not to cry. She wanted to run to Sophie more than anything. To throw her arms around her friend and hold on tight, the way Rom had done with his fellow Cygnian warriors.

A similar reunion wasn't meant for her. It was for the original Hayley. The Hayley they had yet to find.

As if it wasn't enough to be facing down Sophie, Amy and Becca came tearing into the room. Dorn stepped forward, one arm outstretched to block Amy from view partially.

"You shouldn't be here," he said. "It isn't safe."

"It isn't safe for you to be standing between me and my sisters," Amy warned. Another pang swept through Hayley at being included as a sister. Dorn actually dropped his arm and stepped back.

"Wait," Becca said, grabbing Amy's arm. "Something's wrong."

Leave it to Becca to assess a situation in seconds and have a better idea of what was going on than anyone else in the room. Hayley stepped out from under Rom's arm, felt his warmth and encouragement at her back. Drawing on his strength, she found her own. Found just enough to speak.

"Hayley?" Becca whispered.

"No." Hayley shook her head. "I'm not."

"But…" Sophie kept staring at her. "No. You are. I mean… You're her. Look at her." She gestured toward Hayley, then looked back at her sisters.

"There is a lot going on in the universe," Becca said. "We're learning new things every day, like that little trick you used to get yourself here so fast."

Sophie looked at the destroyed kiosks. "I don't know how I did that. I just… I had to get to her." She turned back to Hayley. "Rom said you were here and you were so close that I just had to get to you. Hayley, tell me it's you."

"I wish I could." Tears flowed down Hayley's cheeks. She swiped them away. Rom stepped closer, his hands resting on her shoulders and his reassuring chest at her back. "But I'm not her. I wish I was. But I'm not."

"She's her own person," Rom said, his voice daring anyone to disagree. "Just because she's not the Hayley you know doesn't mean she's not still herself. She's still… her own Hayley."

"*I'm sorry I'm not better at making sense of this,*" Rom thought to her. "*I can only imagine how hard it is for you. Just know that I love you and I'm here for you. I hope that's enough.*"

Hayley reached up and clasped one of his hands. "*It is. I love you, too.*"

"I don't understand," Sophie said.

"Oh no." Becca's eyes widened briefly, then narrowed again. Her jaw set in that way she had that let Hayley know Becca meant business.

Amy saw it and stiffened, glancing warily between Hayley and Sophie. Becca stepped forward and reached toward Sophie's shoulder, but then thought better of it and pulled her hand away. She looked at Lar, who quickly moved in and took her place, wrapping one arm around Sophie's still-crackling back. Becca returned her attention to Hayley.

"I don't know what to say," Becca said. "You know what you are, so you know what Norem did."

"She knows *who* she is," Rom corrected sharply.

"I'm sorry for that," Becca kept addressing Hayley. "He's right. You know... who you are. But I don't. I honestly... I don't know how to deal with this."

Hayley let out a mirthless laugh. "Neither do I."

"I'm about to deal with it by electrocuting everyone in the room," Sophie said. "Except Amy and the dog. And only not Amy because she's carrying my nephew in there."

"Think, Sophie," Becca said. "We just defeated the Norem on Centaurus-10. But he wasn't the only Norem."

"Right, he was a clone—" Sophie's eyes widened and her mouth dropped open. "Wait. No. No!" She shook her head, backing away. Hayley felt each step like a blow.

"I'm so sorry," Hayley said. "I wish I was her. You

have no idea how much I wish I was really her."

"You're you." Rom wrapped his arms around her and pulled her close. "That's more than enough."

Hayley shut her eyes, not wanting to see the grief on the others' faces. On faces she still looked on with sisterly love, even if it didn't belong to her. She knew it wasn't her fault, but she felt like a thief, as if she had stolen something from the original Hayley.

"I would give it back." Hayley dug into her pocket and pulled out the charm bracelet. Stepping forward, away from Rom's embrace, she said, "The memories. The... Everything. I would give it all back, if I could."

Keeping her eyes on the ground, she held the bracelet up for one of them to take. For anyone to take. She didn't want it anymore. The pain of memories that weren't hers, of a future, of a life that she wouldn't have. She knew she'd make a different one with Rom. She knew she would find happiness. But having another woman's memories, dreams, her very identity stamped on her braincells, was more than she could take in that moment. Here was a family, people she felt she had a history with, who she felt she belonged with, but it was a lie. It would always be a lie.

"I would trade places with her in a heartbeat to have her here with you instead of it being me," Hayley said.

"Are there others?" Becca asked. "Others... like you?"

"Not according to Norem's records," Hayley said.

"None that survived."

Becca hissed in a breath, her jaw clenched tight. She put her hands on her hips and stared up at the ceiling. Hayley was certain she was counting to ten to cool off. Maybe twenty.

"He gave you her memories," Becca finally said.

Hayley nodded.

"Did he tell you?" Sophie asked.

"Tell me what?" Hayley still kept her eyes averted, unable to see her best friend looking at her as if she was a stranger.

"Did he tell you … you're a clone?" Sophie said. "Or did he let you believe you were her?"

Hayley let out a harsh breath. "It's Norem. What do you think?"

Sophie stepped forward, her palm beneath Hayley's. She grasped the charm bracelet, her matching one clinking from the movement. Both of them stared at it for a long moment before Hayley finally forced herself to let go.

As the charm bracelet hit Sophie's palm, she reached out and clasped Hayley's hand. The contact was too much. Fresh tears streamed down Hayley's face.

"Look at me," Sophie said. "Please."

Hayley shook her head, gathering her strength. She looked up, locking her gaze with Sophie's. Everything she feared was there. The pain, the fear for her friend—for her real friend—and worst of all, the longing. Sophie stared into Hayley's eyes intensely, searching for her best friend. No matter what she saw there, Hayley would never be the person she was looking for. That Hayley was someone else.

Sophie's grip tightened. "In second grade, you broke mom's favorite figurine. The one of the little clown."

"We all know you did that, Sophie," Amy said. "Dad said you hated that thing."

"She didn't break it," Hayley said quickly.

"You were so scared that my parents would stop letting us play together," Sophie said. "But you still broke it for me. Why?"

Hayley shook her head, trying not to think about the other woman's memories. It almost seemed to be an invasion of privacy at this point, especially about something so important to her.

"Tell me," Sophie said.

"I can't," Hayley said.

"Because you don't remember?" Sophie questioned matter-of-factly. She almost seemed to be taunting Hayley, baiting her. Sophie had always known how to push Hayley's buttons.

"Because you swore me to secrecy." Hayley shook her head. "Swore *her* to secrecy."

"I release you from your promise," Sophie said.

"You can't do that because I'm not her," Hayley shouted. "I won't make choices for her when she's not here."

"Mom knew the truth," Becca said. "She knew about the nightmares."

"She what?" Sophie and Hayley both turned to Becca, speaking at the same time and with the same inflection. Hayley frowned, but she didn't miss the way Sophie's mouth turned up at one corner.

"She knew that you were having nightmares," Becca said. "And she knew that's why Hayley broke the figurine for you."

"She knew that?" Sophie said. "Why didn't she say anything?"

"Because she also knew how much it meant to you both to have a friend like that," Becca said. "Someone who's ride or die. She didn't want to get in the middle of it. She wanted you to have each other. What none of us understood was why that clown figure scared you so badly."

"It was because we snuck off and rode our bikes to that festival I wanted to go to so much," Sophie said. "Hayley found out my plan and insisted on coming with me. When we got there, I ended up getting spooked by one of the clowns, and I twisted my ankle. We hid my bike, and Hayley peddled me back on hers. And then we went back for it a couple weeks later when my ankle was better."

"Mom and Dad would have killed you," Amy said, a gleeful hint to her voice that made Hayley wonder if she was going to rat out her sister, even years later.

"That's how you sprained your ankle?" Becca said. "You made up some shit about some guy named Stevie Renard pushing you down and stealing your bike."

"Johnny," Hayley corrected. Both women looked at her. "It was Johnny Renard."

Becca smirked. "Yeah, it was."

"Who stole her bike," Hayley said quickly.

"You're still sticking to the story after all this time," Becca said.

Hayley pinched her mouth shut. Her heart was aching from the exchange. She didn't want to relive memories that didn't belong to her. Especially with the people involved. People that she still loved as if all those things really had happened to her.

Sophie stepped closer, squaring herself off in front of Hayley. Rom's presence was a reassuring warmth at her back.

"You asked what I think," Sophie said. "What do I think about Norem? I think we're going to find him. And we're going to make him pay for every movie night we missed. We're going to kick his ass so hard, every single one of him is going to feel it. And then we're going to bring you home."

Hayley felt more tears flow down her cheeks. She wasn't sure what Sophie meant, didn't let herself hope, until Sophie pulled her forward and wrapped her arms around her in a crushing embrace.

"We're going to bring both of you home," Sophie whispered.

Chapter Eighteen

"So, let me get this straight." Nancy had been fluttering around Hayley and Katie like a supercharged butterfly, taking charge of all their needs herself, even though every single Cygnian warrior and their soulmates were in the circular common room aboard the *Arrow* and ready to help. Thanks to Nancy, both women were clean, dressed in comfortable clothes, and enjoying a nourishing meal, all in an extraordinarily short amount of time. Rom had never met anyone so efficient—except perhaps her soulmate, Tarn.

"Rom and this Hayley are going to take the *Arrow* while Zakarri and Mindy take his ship to look for Not-Here-Hayley, and they're going to like triangulate her location using their telepathic connection to her," Nancy said. She pointed at the Scorpiian who was standing against the wall as far from the others as he could get. Mindy was enjoying her own meal at his feet.

"And where the *Arrow* goes, I go," Tarn said.

"And where you go, I go." Nancy sauntered over to her soulmate, smiling. When she reached him, she leaned against his chest. He bent down so she could pull herself up on her tip-toes and rub their noses together.

It was weird. Kind of cute, but… deeply weird.

Hayley was smiling at the exchange. Maybe Rom would have to try rubbing his nose against hers at some point to see if she liked it. Earthlings abounded with odd gestures of affection.

"Meanwhile, the Centauran vessel that we captured will be turned over to the Vegans so that they can analyze its technology," Lar said.

"I still think we should give it to the Coalition," Sophie said. "The Centaurans have taken so much from the Sadirians. It's time they gave something back."

"If you give the ship to the Coalition, it will be seen as an act of war," Dean—no, Zakarri said.

"And you would know all about those," Sophie snapped.

Zakarri nodded. "That's why you should listen to me."

"Or," Nancy broke in loudly, "we could give it back to the Centaurans. As a gesture of goodwill. I mean, technically, I'm a Centauran now myself. I could be an ambassador or something."

"That is actually not a bad idea," Becca said.

Nancy beamed. "Seriously? Wait, the returning the ship part or the ambassador part?"

Becca ignored the question, turning to Kral instead. "Since the ship was damaged by a Cygnian, we should probably repair it before returning it."

"Absolutely." Kral grinned, baring his teeth as he did in anticipation of a particularly enjoyable battle. "And since it's a design we're unfamiliar with, we'll have to ask our allies, the Vegans, to assist with this."

"Better be sure to get our own scans as well," Becca suggested. "In case we run across any other Centauran vessels that need help in the future."

"Being an ambassador between Cygnians and Centaurans is going to be hard, isn't it..." Nancy said, her smile falling.

Rom laughed, shifting next to Hayley so that he could hold her closer against his side while she ate. Her eyes sparkled with energy, and her cheeks still held their color. Nuar, their medic, had examined Hayley, Katie, and Mindy and said they were all fine. They needed to get back to Cyan and let her do her own exam, though. The Vegan xenobiologist would be able to use her advanced technology to make much more sense of whatever Norem might have done to them.

"Our first step is for Lar, Sophie, Tarn, and Nancy to pilot the Centauran ship back to Earth," Kral said. "Tarn, see if you can get their cloak working. I don't want to raise the alarm if anyone sees a Centauran vessel approaching, even if it's with the *Arrow*."

"Understood," Tarn said.

"As soon as we get everyone checked out, we can begin our rescue mission," Kral said.

"We're heading out now." Zakarri stepped away from the wall.

"What?" Hayley said.

Mindy hurried over to Hayley and jumped up to lick her chin. *"I'll check in with you every day. Twice a day. Our connection is clear and I'm stronger now."*

"I'm still going to miss you," Hayley thought. Rom could feel her keeping a tight hold on her emotions, not wanting to trouble Mindy with them.

"I'll miss you, too, but it's only for a little while," Mindy thought back. *"Just till we find first-friend-Hayley."*

She gave Hayley one more kiss, then trotted back over to sit next to Zakarri.

"Mindy needs to be examined by Cyan, too," Kral said. "We don't know the extent of her modifications. There could be complications you don't foresee."

"Life is filled with unforeseen complications," Zakarri conceded. "Mindy and I are in agreement. I've seen her files, and she's heard Norem speak of her enough that we're certain she's in no danger. We won't wait a moment longer before looking for Hayley."

"It's what Mindy wants to do," Hayley confirmed.

"I can't believe it, but I agree with him," Sophie said. "I don't want to leave Hayley out there with Norem. Other Hayley," she added, glancing at Hayley apologetically.

"Let's make this a little easier for everyone," Hayley said. "I can go by my middle name, Lynn."

"Are you sure?" Sophie said. "You never really liked that name."

"My perspective has kind of shifted on a lot of things," Hayley said. "I'm kind of loving everything about Hayley now. And this is a way to simplify things." She glanced up at Rom. "Are you okay with that?"

"I will call you whatever you want me to," Rom said. "Lynn."

She smiled, her cheeks flushing. "Okay, now I really like that name. Especially when you say it."

"Time to sound-proof another bedroom," Tarn said.

"Might want to do the same for engineering." Bron, the only Cygnian cyborg in existence grinned at his best friend.

"Oh... Really?" Nancy's face turned bright red. "Sorry about that."

"Focus, people," Nuar's soulmate, Lian yelled. She stared around the room and said, "What were we talking about? This damn pregnancy brain..."

Nuar sat next to her and handed her a fresh bowl of ice cream. "We were talking about how the others learned of the need for sound-proofing after you moved into my quarters with me."

Lian scowled at him, before she smirked. She turned back to her ice cream, scooting closer to him on the bench seat where they sat.

"If I can jump in with an 'unforeseen complication' of

my own," Katie began, "I'd like to go with Dean and Mindy. I mean Zakarri and Mindy. Dammit, everybody needs to pick just one name and stick with it."

"I work alone," Zakarri said.

"And see where that's gotten you." Olivia's low, quiet voice somehow always commanded attention. She stared up at Zakarri with eyes that glowed the same blue as her soulmate, Bron's, now that she carried their children.

Mindy looked up at him and whined, her tail thumping on the floor where she sat. He scratched her head, staring at her intently. Rom was certain they were communicating, but he wasn't privy to their conversation this time.

"I can help you," Katie said. "I don't think the late Norem had a chance to let the others know about my abilities. Get me close to his tech, and he won't know what hit him."

Zakarri scowled. "You're really going to trust yourself with the most notorious criminal in the galaxy?"

"If I trust you with a dog, I trust you with myself," Katie said, laughing.

Nancy leaned closer and loudly whispered, "He likes animals more than people."

Katie leaned forward and mimicked her whisper. "A lot of people like animals more than people."

Rom swore he saw Zakarri's lips twitch up in a smirk. He was pretty certain that group would be okay. He was still a little worried about Hayley—Lynn. Her nervousness rang clearly through their bond. Not about their mission to find Hayley, but about heading back to Earth.

He leaned in and said, "What's bothering you?"

"I was just wondering what David and Shannon will think of all this," Lynn said. "What will they think of me?"

Sophie plopped down beside her on the bench and threw her arm over Lynn's shoulders. "Mom and Dad will think what I do. What we all do."

"Which is?" Lynn hesitantly asked.

Sophie pulled Lynn closer. "How lucky we are that now we get to love the two of you, twins."

Lynn burst into tears, wrapping her arms around Sophie's neck. The next thing Rom knew, he was being nudged out of the way as Amy and Becca joined them in their embrace.

Becca nuzzled Lynn's head and said, "You're family. Nothing gets in the way of that."

He gave them another moment, then said, "Not that I'm trying to get in the way of anything, but I'd really like to take my soulmate to our quarters so she can get some rest." He took Lynn's hand and helped her to her feet.

"Sure," Amy said. "'Rest.'"

"Amy," Lynn chided.

"'Lynn and Rom, sitting in—'" Amy began, in a sing-song voice.

"Shut it!" Sophie clamped her hand over Amy's mouth, playfully pushing her onto her side on the bench. Amy promptly reached up and stuck her fingers between Sophie's ribs, making her shriek with laughter and roll onto the floor.

"Don't start something if you can't finish it!" Amy said, a broad smile on her face.

Sophie sat up and said, "Oh my god, little sisters are such a pain."

"Little sisters are the best," Lynn said. Sophie reached up and gave her hand a squeeze as they passed.

They were a little ways down the corridor when they heard someone hurrying up behind them. Rom didn't sense the person, so it had to be either Katie… or Zakarri. He turned around, somewhat reassured when the Scorpiian held up his hands in a gesture of peace.

"I just… I need one moment," Zakarri said.

Rom looked to Lynn, who nodded. He stayed close, but took a step back to give them a little space.

"What is it?" Lynn asked.

"I um…" Zakarri ran his hand through his hair, a nervous gesture Rom had only seen the Scorpiian do in Lynn's presence. "You have her memories," Zakarri said.

"Dean—sorry, Zakarri…" she began. "I can't tell you things that she doesn't want you to know. It's not my place."

"I know," he said. "I get that. I'm not asking about anything that happened before. And I know that I've ruined our chance for…" He glanced up at Rom and shook his head. "For something like what you have. I just want to know if you think... Do you think she can ever forgive me? Because I don't think I can ever forgive myself if she can't." Silver liquid pooled in his eyes, until he blinked it away quickly.

Rom couldn't believe it, but he felt for the guy. If he had had a chance with someone like Lynn, someone full of caring and honor and with such strength and compassion, he didn't know if he'd ever recover if he messed it up. Especially as profoundly as Zakarri had.

Lynn took a deep breath, then let it out. "I think that you both need to realize that what's happened to her—what's... what's still happening—is Norem's doing. He's the one who's hurting people. But, you've hurt people as well. You have a lot to atone for."

Zakarri nodded. "Yeah. I get that."

"Maybe while you're looking for her, you should start trying to make some of that right," Lynn said. "At least, what you can."

He nodded again. "Thanks."

"Sure."

Zakarri took a step back, but Lynn rushed forward and hugged him. His eyes widened in surprise. Then he hugged her back, a brief moment of peace washing over his features. He released her and stepped away again, his eyes downcast.

He nodded and said, "Good luck to you both. I really

mean that."

"Good luck to you," Rom said. "You're going to need it out there."

Zakarri briefly met his steady look. He gave a curt nod, then turned and was gone.

"I think I've used up all of the adrenaline my body can ever make for emotionally charged exchanges," Lynn said. "Can we please go take a nap now?"

"Absolutely." Rom swept her up into his arms, then turned and headed down the corridor. He leaned in, never breaking his stride, and said, "You sure you want to sleep right away though?"

Lynn laughed, the care-free sound something he wasn't sure he'd ever hear from her, let alone this soon. He counted himself among the luckiest men in the universe to hear it, to hold this exceptional woman in his arms.

He would never let her go.

Epilogue

Centauran Exploratory Vessel
Sector Nine

"This is the last Centauran ship I can secure for you." Paxel, the most weaselly Tau Ceti Hayley had ever encountered, handed an ID pad to Norem.

"It's the last one I'll need," Norem said.

"I mean it," Paxel said. "Something is brewing with our 'allies.' They're growing suspicious, especially of anything involving you."

"Well, in a few more months, I'll be able to share my research with them." Norem smiled. "Then their suspicions will be ended—along with their lives."

Paxel laughed. "You always did have too high of an opinion of yourself."

"I think my opinion is just about as high as it should be." Norem pressed his palm against the ID pad, holding it there until a green light flashed.

"You know, this is a big ship." Paxel took back the ID pad. He held his hand above its screen, but didn't press it. "You bringing on a crew?"

'So close...' Hayley thought. *'Come on...'*

"I don't need a crew," Norem said. "Although, an update from my colleagues would be nice," he muttered under his breath."

"What's that?" Paxel said.

"Nothing. All I need is H-0. I've finished the last augmentation. Now it's just a matter of waiting for it to set so that I can implant the final memories and programming. She'll be able to run everything for me."

She can already run everything. She just needs the final access codes.

Paxel stared up at Hayley, squinting at her through the viscous liquid. She kept her eyelids nearly closed, staring through the tiniest slit between them and keeping her eyelids motionless. Norem thought she was unconscious, unaware of everything going on around her. She needed him to keep thinking that for just a little while longer.

The last augmentation had been a game changer. Norem thought he was using some kind of neural link to make it easier to program her cybernetics and download whatever brainwashing programs he wanted to install in her mind based on a test run with someone he called K-0. Instead, Hayley had come out of her last fever-state able to control technology with the power of thought.

She had managed to alter a memory upload from one of the other Norem clones, warning him to remove the programming after discovering that it had done a lot more than make it easier for organic minds to communicate with cybernetics. Hayley had made it sound harmless. Successful, even. She had kept her new abilities quiet, only practicing when she was alone. Small tests.

This was the final exam.

"Whatever you say." Paxel sneered, obviously unconvinced. He pressed his hand to the ID pad.

Hayley didn't let herself hold her breath. She kept her vitals absolutely stable, even though her heart wanted to race, her palms wanted to sweat and her lungs wanted to lock in every molecule of oxygen. One of the benefits of being half machine was the ability to keep all of her autonomic systems functioning not-so-autonomically.

She waited.

This would be it. She would send part of her consciousness through the circuits in the tank where she floated. Glowing yellow circuit boards would light up as her awareness flowed through them, turning green as she made them her own. The narrow corridor of electric conduits would open up into a huge horizon, just as it did in her practices with the Tau Ceti ship Norem had kept them on before this one. She would soar into the black void of endless possibilities stretching above her, her mind's eye looking down at the mainframe of the ship.

Norem would be confused when he heard the ship speak of departure orders. He would turn and look at her with dread that turned to fear that turned to terror as her tank drained at his feet. Her eyes would open slowly, and just as he had greeted her every time he let her gain consciousness over the last few torturous months, she would say, '*Hello, Norem,*' and then smash through the tank and kill him.

Morbid delight skittered through her. All she needed was for the transfer of ship's functions to be completed and she could—

The moment the light on the ID pad turned green, Norem lashed out with his arm, punching Paxel in the stomach. No, not punching him... impaling him.

Her heart thundered, her eyes flying open. All her careful self-control fled as she saw the light glinting off of what looked like a silver spear tip sticking out of Paxel's back. Norem caught the ID pad as it fell, letting Paxel's lifeless body slide to the floor. Only, now it wasn't Norem.

His skin rippled with silver light that she had once thought beautiful. Now, it only filled her with rage. His features morphed into soft lips, strong jaw, chiseled cheekbones, and expressive eyes. The light faded, leaving his brown hair as unruly as always, his outfit changing to the dark turtleneck and charcoal gray slacks that he knew were her favorite.

His warm chestnut eyes turned to her, eyes filled with so much pain, her heart clenched and she gasped, pulling in extra liquid through the gills in her neck. The gills that wouldn't be there if Norem hadn't had a chance to transform her DNA, adding in physical characteristics from different species as it suited his curiosity. Rage chased away whatever kinder emotions might have tried to rise within her, dousing the flicker of warmth she still felt for this man—this Scorpiian.

Dean...

"Hayley, I'm here. I..." His eyes roved over her and his jaw clenched, a muscle twitching along his cheek. Silver light rippled over his skin again. He took a deep breath and let it out slowly. The rippling stopped. He pressed his free hand to the tank, stepping closer.

"It's over," he said, his voice filled with an intensity that sent a shiver over her. "No one will ever hurt you again."

If only that were true. Floating in the tank, staring at him, all the feelings she had pushed aside came rushing back. The excitement of their budding relationship. The thrill of the thought of going into space. The deep connection that she swore she had felt building between them.

And the way it had all ended.

Hayley closed her eyes, unable to look at the man who had given her so much hope and caused her so much pain. She forced her traitorous heart to slow, reminded herself that even though Norem took much from her, he had also given her power. More power than anyone realized.

But they would learn, starting with the man who had

broken her heart. Starting with Dean.

—

WAIT!!! I know you're upset. I said Rom's story would be the last book in the *Cygnian 7* series. But that was *before*. Before Hayley turned out to be Hayley's clone and Dean/Zakarri earned himself a redemption arc. That was before Tobek earned his place as an honorary Cygnian warrior. It was certainly before so many of my readers emailed me asking if I could please, please, *please* write more *Cygnian 7* books. Well, buckle up, readers, because things are about to become a lot more intense! And read on for a sneak peek at the book no one expected, but everybody wanted…

Zakarri: A Cygnian Allies Romance

Cygnian 7

Book Eight

(I know, right???)

Chapter One

This wasn't the way things were supposed to happen. None of it was.

Hayley was suspended in a tank of yellow-green liquid, staring out at the face of a man she had once thought she might love. A man who had handed her over to a mad Tau Ceti scientist named Norem and then left her to be experimented on.

Aliens, all of them. And now, she was one, too, even to herself.

No, she was worse than an alien. She was some sort of Frankenstein's monster. DNA had been spliced into her genome, giving her gills and blue-tinged skin. Parts of her body had been *removed* and replaced with mechanisms. After hacking into Norem's computer files, she had learned what they had removed from her had been reclassified as 'materials.' Been used in still more experiments, cloning projects, DNA modification of other individuals, other people. They were hurting her—maiming her—and the results were enabling them to hurt even more people.

That all ended now.

The idiots had been trying to create a stronger super soldier. Their successes had far surpassed their grandiose expectations, and they'd never realized it. She had the strength of a Cygnian warrior, as well as some of their invulnerabilities. Hayley had the amphibious nature of the Tau Ceti, along with their ability to cling to vertical and horizontal surfaces—at least, with her remaining organic hand and foot. She could magnetize her cybernetic limbs and stick to metal surfaces even more effectively.

Thanks to her latest enhancement—an augmentation implanted in her brain that was intended to make it easier for the Tau Ceti to integrate autonomous control of her cybernetics—she could access any computer near enough to her and take control of it. She'd been exceedingly careful so far, not wanting them to realize how screwed the Tau Ceti were. Hayley had wanted a few more enhancements and tweaks before she started to wreak havoc on Norem and everyone who had ever shaken hands with him.

It had been all too easy to alter the programming of the nanites they had infused into her system. They only obeyed *her* now and had been modifying the mechanisms implanted in her body, at her command. She had switched out schematics so that the scientists experimenting on her were actually installing all the requisite parts she needed for her nanites to create weapons, shields and life support systems that would help her survive even in the vacuum of space.

She had a long 'TBD' wishlist—'to be destroyed.' Things were going to get messy.

Norem was at the top of her list. She had wanted him to

be the first person she ended. The only person she thought she could bring herself to kill.

After months of torture, Hayley had dreamed of nothing else but taking down the man responsible for her pain. She had intended to kill Norem herself, but Dean had beaten her to it. Yet another thing the shape-shifting mercenary had stolen from her. This Scorpiian was equally culpable for the horrors she'd suffered at the hands of the Tau Ceti. She should have added Dean to her TBD list long ago.

For all she cared, Dean could take Norem's place in her fantasies. In the end, all that mattered was that she would be free.

Dean stood before her, eyes glittering with quicksilver, his face a mask of despair. If she didn't know better, she'd think his heart had been broken, just as hers had been. Except, she did know better. Dean didn't have a heart. He was a cold, cruel, ruthless mercenary. She'd be doing the universe an immense favor by ending him.

Norem had installed her tank in a laboratory in the most recent ship he'd acquired for them. His extreme paranoia was well founded. The Centaurans who had allied themselves with the Tau Ceti were finally beginning to realize the error of their decision. Norem was the Tau Ceti's lead scientist. He was becoming careless, letting details slip that raised Centauran suspicions about him experimenting on sentient life forms. The Centaurans would have killed him themselves if they'd had solid facts instead of mere hints and suspicions in regard to what he was doing. Instead, they'd given him yet another ship.

Given *her* a ship.

Hayley's command to the ship's computer opened the grate at the bottom of her tank. The liquid began to drain. Dean's eyes widened. Her body slowly drifted downward as the tank emptied. Finally, her feet rested on its base. Clenching her left hand— the metal hand attached to her metal arm, thanks to Norem—into a fist, she pulled it back. The look of astonishment on Dean's face made her smile.

"Hello, Dean," she said, just before she punched through the transparent side.

The material that made up the tank was the same that they used in the viewports. Supposedly, it could withstand asteroid storms and weapons from other ships. When Hayley struck it, it shattered into a thousand pieces that shot across the floor, showering Dean with shards. Gashes opened up on his face and quicksilver flowed down his cheek before being reabsorbed as the wounds sealed themselves. He kept staring at her, as if he hadn't even noticed the injuries. Hayley would give him some that he couldn't ignore.

Snarling, she leapt forward, readying her arm for another strike. This time, her metal fist connected with his chiseled jaw, sending Dean sprawling back. He staggered, arms flailing to keep his balance. The ship's control pad flew from his hand, sliding across the floor. Hayley didn't care. She didn't require it anymore. The ship was already hers. The computer...

Something was wrong with the computer. There was another presence in the mainframe—another intelligence. An AI?

It didn't matter. She would teach it to obey, right after she finished delivering justice to Dean.

The Scorpiian just kept staring at her with those soulful brown eyes. Not speaking. Not moving. Not reacting. She would move him herself.

She grabbed the front of his shirt—rather, the part of his body made to look like a shirt—and lifted him off his feet before hurling him across the room. He hit the bulkhead with a satisfying crash, sliding to the floor. Before he could stand again, she was on him, her enhanced speed letting her move faster than she had even realized. She braced herself against the wall to help stop her momentum, needing to learn her body while using some of her enhancements for the first time.

"You... took... everything from me!" she screamed, punctuating her words with brutal kicks to Dean's torso. The Scorpiian didn't curl into a ball, didn't make an attempt to defend himself. Was she even hurting him? Could he truly not feel anything at all?

She had thought he loved her. He had *told* her that he

loved her. Another lie. The most egregious of them all.

She grabbed him again, this time, holding him over her head. She could bring him down on her knee, the way she'd seen done in the movies and snap his spine. Except, he would just heal. Where was the satisfaction in that? Scorpiians could change shape at will. He had shared that with her—shown her his true form even—right before dumping her with Norem when she'd had a little mini-freak-out.

Who wouldn't freak out at the prospect of leaving their planet with a boyfriend they had just found out was a shapeshifting Gray? She had only needed time, before—

Before what? Before flying off into the sunset to get our very own 'happily-ever-after?'

Tears blurred her vision. She didn't want that. She had never wanted that.

Now who's lying?

She flung Dean across the room, needing him away from her. He hit the deck in front of the empty tank, rolling over the broken shards. Slowly, he lifted himself onto his hands and knees, turning back to stare at her. The razor sharp shards protruded from wounds that oozed quicksilver.

"Why aren't you healing yourself?" Hayley screeched in frustration. "Why aren't you fighting back?"

His breath rushed out in a gasp that seemed to empty him.

"Because I will do anything to help you through this," Dean said. "So, if this is what you need…" His voice trailed off as his features once more twisted with sorrow.

Her heart tugged at his expression, at his words. He seemed sincere.

He had seemed sincere before.

"I need for you to have been there for me," she screamed, turning to the nearest workstation. She tore it from its moorings and threw it at Dean. He didn't even try to dodge it. The heavy block of metal struck him with an ominous crunch before rolling off of him. He lay flat on the ground, wheezing as his chest struggled to pull in air.

How hurt was he? Was he trapped in that human form? No, she'd seen him change shape earlier. He had shifted from Norem—the most hated form imaginable to her—to this. A face she had once lovingly traced. Arms that had held her close as they ran through rain-soaked streets on a dark night in Paris. The night they met.

I don't want him to die.

What did she want? What did she need from him?

She didn't know, except that it wasn't this.

"Heal yourself," she ordered.

He looked over at her and shook his head, the movement barely perceptible. She stalked closer.

"Heal yourself," she demanded.

Again, he shook his head, more firmly this time. He rolled to his back, wincing as he stared at the ceiling.

"I deserve this," he wheezed painfully. "This and more."

"Dammit, Dean."

Hayley reached down and hefted him to his feet as if he weighed nothing. Sinuous strands of metal snaked out from her left arm, tiny clamps on their ends opening and snapping shut. Piloted by her nanites, the strands roamed over him, plucking the shards from his wounds and cauterizing the worst of them. He took a few more deep, rattling breaths, then closed his eyes. The misshapen part of his chest filled out as he finally healed at least that.

God, she had forgotten how gorgeous he was. His unruly brown hair always looked stylishly windswept. His strong cheekbones and lithe frame made him look as though he'd just stepped out of Hollywood. And those expressive brown eyes... They never failed to make her heart flutter.

Even now.

"Why didn't you come for me?" she whispered shakily.

"I did. By the time I returned to the base, you were already gone."

"I wanted you to save me." Tears escaped her eyes. She hadn't known she could still cry. Dean winced as he watched them roll down her cheek. He reached up to brush them away.

"I wanted to save you, too," he said.

Gently, he dared to clasp her right hand—the one still

made of human flesh. She couldn't bring herself to pull away. He studied her face, his expression tightening as he took in the ports that had been implanted just above her ears, the lines of circuits glowing just beneath her skin that she knew were visible when she was this worked up, the creases in her neck where her gills currently were closed.

"What Norem took from you—" His voice broke and he looked to the floor briefly. When he met her eyes again, his had flooded with silver. "He took *you* from *me*. He took everything *we* could have been. He took... everything, *from us*." Dean blinked, and the quicksilver filling his eyes drained out as tears of his own. "You were my everything, Hayley. You still are."

—

I have been in love with Zakarri since he first showed us his vulnerable side in *Rate of Return*. He's been my favorite thorn in everyone's side for so many books. I think he's finally grown enough to earn his own happily-ever-after. And I know that Hayley certainly deserves hers! My readers have spoken, and their 'happily-ever-after' for this series is for it to continue for a long time. I will do my best to keep providing you with awesome adventures in the Cygnians' universe! Keep an eye out for the unexpected eighth *Cygnian 7* book, *Zakarri: A Cygnian Allies Romance*!

If you want to learn more about Rom and the other Cygnian warriors' universe, you can check out *The Department of Homeworld Security* adventures. Many of the novellas have been collected in the first two series omnibuses, *The Department of Homeworld Security Omnibus 1* and *The Department of Homeworld Security Omnibus 2*. Or you can pick and choose with the individual novellas. You'll want to check out *Nothing to Declare* to see Zakarri's first appearance and *Business or Pleasure* to see how Norem (aka 'Norm') began his evil schemes.

I'd love to keep in touch. Join my newsletter at cassandra-chandler.com to hear about all the adventures happening in Cassland. And if you enjoyed this book, please consider leaving a review at your favorite book review site. I'd really appreciate it—reviews help readers and authors alike!

Thank you for reading *Rom: A Scifi Alien Warriors Romance!*

Cassandra Chandler

About the Author

USA Today Bestselling author Cassandra Chandler uses her vivid imagination to make the world more interesting, spawning the ideas she turns into her captivating Science Fiction Romances and enthralling Paranormal and Urban Fantasy Romances. Fast-paced and funny, lighthearted or filled with suspense, her stories will introduce you to characters you'll fall in love with and worlds you long to explore.

www.ingramcontent.com/pod-product-compliance
Lightning Source LLC
Chambersburg PA
CBHW071327250626
47159CB00004B/1500